# Ineligible

Bijaya Kumar Mishra

Invincible Publishers

First published in India in 2018



ISBN: 978-93-88333-33-7



Invincible Publishers

G-120, Sushant Lok III, Sector 57, Gurgaon-122002

Registered Address: Opposite Kasturba Ashram, Radaur, Haryana–135133

Printed at Thomson Press (India) LTD

*To those who dare to have extraordinary expectations.*

# Acknowledgements

This book is the result of the efforts and good wishes of a number of people. I would like to thank:

All my readers who chose to read this book.

Mr. Ajay Setia, for his consistent help during the publishing process.

My editor, Aditi Saxena, for her dedicated effort to refine the manuscript.

The publishing crew – Anjali Arya, Ashish Samant, Ruchika Khanna and others – without whose hard work this book wouldn't be in my readers' hands.

My family, for supporting me selflessly at all times during my writing journey.

My friends who have always encouraged me to progress further in the world of writing.

*Disclaimer*

# Chapter 1

Saahil came out of the library and drove off in his brand new sedan. After ten minutes, he drove past a flower garden which was emitting a sweet fragrance, and reached his mansion. He lifted his brand new sedan to the corridor on the first floor of his mansion, and chained its rear wheel to the railing in order to prevent it from getting stolen. The thoughts of Varsha were playing hide and seek in his mind – her wavy hair...blue eyes...enigmatic smile…and the kiss that she had given him.

He heard some nice music being played somewhere. But soon, the music grew louder and louder, then got distorted gradually until it turned into a fusion of shouts and complaints. It was Sakku *bai* with her daily ritual of complaints – 'I won't wash Vaibhav sahab's stinky socks…The price of pumpkin has hiked by another two rupees. How will I get pumpkin for Munna if you people don't increase my salary? The watchman always stares and smiles at me slyly. Tell him that's not right…' She added the last complaint with such a shy smile that Saahil couldn't decide whether it was a complaint or an affirmative message for the watchman.

Finally, the watchman's stares, Vaibhav's stinky socks and Munna's pumpkins won over Varsha's blue eyes and wavy hair, and brought Saahil back to his senses. He realized that he wasn't in any mansion, but was standing in the first floor corridor of the working men's hostel. Sakku *bai,* the hostel maid, was shouting and waving her broom like a sword, making dust particles fly all over the place. Saahil sneezed twice, then looked at his brand new sedan, only to realize that it had transformed back into his old second hand bicycle, the rear wheel of which was chained to the railing of the corridor. The flower garden he had crossed just before reaching his hostel was nothing but the local fish market, stinking of rotten fish. He realized that it was the thoughts of Varsha that had waved a magic wand and converted his gloomy world into one full of charm and ecstasy.

Nothing irritated Saahil at that moment. He smiled at Sakku *bai* and said, 'Life will become more beautiful if you just stop complaining.'

'But pumpkin is so costly these days, you know?' Sakku bai waved her broom again.

Instead of participating in the pumpkin debate, Saahil entered his room, the door of which was guarded partly by termites and spiders, and partly by pictures of scantily clad models and actresses. He lounged carefully on his bed, the fourth leg of which had been replaced by a pile of bricks.

He saw Vaibhav, his roommate, struggling with a mound of dirty clothes and some books lying haphazardly on his bed. Vaibhav's choice of books was as weird as his nature. Saahil saw cockroaches and spiders creep around over old calendars, damp walls and termite-damaged windows. There were empty packets of cigarettes and empty bottles of alcohol lying on the floor, re-telling the stories of the various parties held in the past.

'Disgusting. Everything is just so disgusting,' Saahil thought and closed his eyes.

As soon as he did, Varsha smiled at him in the darkness.

'No. Everything is not disgusting. There are beautiful people like Varsha who make this world a beautiful place to live in. And beautiful people do beautiful things like…like kissing people,' Saahil said to himself and smiled. He caressed his own cheek, trying to cherish the touch of Varsha's lips. 'Yes. She did kiss me. Yes. Varsha kissed me.'

'Varsha kissed you?' Vaibhav was standing near Saahil's bed, his eyes and mouth wide open in surprise.

Saahil rose from his bed in shock. 'Who told you?'

'You said it just now.'

Saahil realized that he had actually said it out loud for Vaibhav to hear. 'You are not going to tell this to anyone, right?'

Vaibhav had a cunning smile on his face. 'I would love to keep it a secret. But, my stomach starts aching if I keep a lot of secrets in it, you know?'

'A can of beer will be enough to keep your stomach ache in control, I suppose.'

'It won't work. Suboptimal dose. Make it two.'

'Okay. Done. You are a greedy, insatiable monster.'

'Thanks for the compliment. Now tell me everything that happened between Varsha and you.'

Saahil said, 'You know Das uncle, the librarian, who helped me deal with the various complexities of my orphanhood -he's helping me earn some money these days by providing me with petty projects and thesis related work for college students. I help him in his work, and manage the library in his absence. Today, he went outside for a while and I was standing alone at the reception counter of the library. At the moment, Varsha rushed in and asked me to let her hide somewhere. So I let her hide behind the bookshelves.'

'Why did she need to hide?' Vaibhav asked.

'She said Naina was after her. You know Naina, don't you?'

'Yes. Naina is infamous for being skeptical about everyone and everything. While buying a packet of cookies, she asks the salesman to weigh the packet and cross-check the weight with that written on the packet. After buying a new deodorant, she tries it on her pet cat first. After all, the CEO of the deodorant company might have conspired to harm her beautiful skin. She got an amulet from a saint and has given it to her boyfriend. It is supposed to keep her boyfriend away from other girls. But why was she after Varsha?'

'Naina wants to marry Varsha's pet dog, Aryan. And Varsha doesn't want to let Aryan marry Naina,' Saahil replied.

'What…? Naina wants to marry Varsha's pet dog? So weird!'

'Not for Naina. A saint, who had returned from the Himalayas, had told her that her first husband would die after their wedding, so she should marry a dog first. The dog, being her first husband, would die after the wedding, and Naina could marry her boyfriend later without any risk to his life. So, she was after Varsha in order to get Aryan.'

'Why Aryan? Why not just any stray dog?' Vaibhav asked.

'Naina wouldn't want to marry someone who doesn't have class,' Saahil replied.

Both Vaibhav and Saahil laughed.

'What happened next?' Vaibhav was curious.

'Naina came to the library searching for Varsha, but couldn't find her. So she left. Then, Varsha came out of her hiding and kissed me on the cheek as a gesture of thanks. I gathered the courage to tell her that she had beautiful and talkative eyes. She said that I would soon discover she had talkative hands too. I don't know why she said that. Then, she smiled mysteriously, shook hands with me and left. I still can't believe she really kissed me.'

'Yes. It's difficult to believe that one of the loveliest girls in college kissed a nobody like you. But it's just destiny. It's all written in your palms.'

Saahil didn't mind Vaibhav calling him a nobody as he was well versed with Vaibhav's weird manners. Nevertheless, he knew that Vaibhav was the only friend he could count on in any situation. He said, 'You are right. It's all written in our palms.'

'But what's written in your palm?' Vaibhav asked.

'How would I know? I am not a palmist.'

'Nor am I. But right now, I can read your destiny written on your palm and it says that you are in love.'

'What do you mean?'

'Don't act innocent. Anyone can read what you have written on your palm.'

Saahil looked at his palms and discovered another hard-to-believe surprise. For a moment, he thought someone had done some sort of sorcery. He had no idea how the words had appeared on his right palm. The words written in faint blue were very common, yet the most magical – 'I love you.' Saahil struggled for words, 'I…I…you know...I mean, I have not written it.'

'Who has written it then?'

'I have no idea.'

Vaibhav guffawed. 'Are you a man or a graffiti wall? Can anyone come and write on you, while you have no idea who has done it? Strange. But the strangest thing is that Varsha kissed you for doing her such a small favor – just for allowing her to hide somewhere. Are you sure that was the only reason why she kissed you?'

'Definitely…perhaps…at least she said so. Why?'

'Because Varsha doesn't give kisses to boys in charity. She is one of the most decent girls in college.'

Saahil stood silent, but the man inside him was restless and happy and doubtful and euphoric and infatuated and intrigued and confused, all at the same time.

He spent the day watching his six-legged and eight-legged roommates creep across the old calendars, damp walls and termite-infested windows. His heart kept suggesting explanations. His mind kept asking for evidences. The night was even tougher. Unable to sleep, he came out of his room and started loitering in the corridor. He wondered why Varsha had said that she had talkative hands.

Suddenly, his foot slipped on something and he caught hold of one of the pillars in the corridor to balance himself. He left an impression of his palm on the pillar, which had been painted recently and was still wet. He should have gotten irritated. But no, he didn't. Instead, he looked at the paint on his palm and the impression of his palm on the pillar, and a big grin appeared on his face. He rushed back to his room and shook Vaibhav vigorously by his arms. 'Wake up, wake up.'

'What happened?' Vaibhav woke up with a jerk.

'I want to shake hands with you.'

Vaibhav looked at the wall clock, the seconds hand of which had taken retirement from its service long ago, and asked, 'Are you mad or a moron? You woke me up at four in the morning to shake hands with me?'

Saahil ignored his question, shook hands with him and said, 'See, your palm got stained with the paint that was on my palm when I shook hands with you.'

'Wow! Wow! What a great discovery! What a great discovery! We can call it "Saahil's theory of transfer of paint." I am sure you will get some award for this great discovery of yours some day. Now, can I go back to sleep?'

'No. I have got something to tell you. Her hands are talkative too.'

'What?'

'Varsha said that her hands were talkative too. Now I know what she had meant. Perhaps, she had written "I love you" on her palm before shaking hands with me. When we shook hands, the words got imprinted onto my palm. She was too shy to tell me directly what she felt about me. So, her hands did the talking.' Saahil had a big smile on his face.

Vaibhav's sleep dissolved completely. He sat awestruck for a few minutes. Then he said, 'Logically, I should disagree with you, but my sixth sense says that you are right. Perhaps Varsha loves you.'

'I need to confirm that. You know Varsha, right? Can you arrange a meeting with her?' Saahil said.

'I will try. But answer my question first. Let's assume that Varsha loves you. But do you love her?'

'I don't know. But I have started to love the feeling of being loved. An orphan like me knows the real value of love. Please arrange my meeting with Varsha.'

'I will try. Now, let me sleep.' Vaibhav went back to sleep. Saahil went back to watching his six-legged and eight-legged roommates creep around.

The next day, Vaibhav took Saahil to a restaurant and said, 'I have asked Varsha to come here. She will be here in a few minutes. I am leaving now.'

'No. Wait. How can you leave me alone? See, I am already sweating. My hands are trembling. My heart is beating so fast. I am so nervous,' Saahil said.

'Enjoy the feeling. The monster of first love scares you only once in your life. It's a fear that you can enjoy,' Vaibhav said and left.

Saahil tried to calm himself down as he waited for Varsha. To his surprise, all his nervousness vanished as Varsha came and sat opposite him. Their lips started showering smiles.

After they had ordered two cups of coffee, Varsha said, 'Vaibhav said you wanted to meet me.' She was unable to suppress the smile on her lips.

Saahil said, 'I wanted you to know that I liked what your talkative hands said to me.'

'I was afraid the ink might get dry before we shook hands.'

Saahil was more than delighted. 'That means my guess was correct? That means you...you really love me?'

Varsha looked down and said, ‘Why do you boys always want to hear it directly from girls?’

‘No. I mean, I still can’t believe that you love me. We hardly know each other...’

‘Wrong. You hardly know me. But I know everything about you. I have always felt it about you. But I had never been able to catch your attention.’

‘That means all that happened in the library was pre-planned. Right?’

‘Nothing was pre-planned. When I was hiding behind the bookshelves, it occurred to me that if I didn’t do something at that moment to express my feelings for you, I wouldn’t ever be able to do so. So I wrote those words on my palm then and there,’ Varsha said shyly.

‘But why me? I am an orphan. I don’t have a house. I don’t have money. I don’t even have a job, though I have already graduated. I am no match for you. Then why me?’

‘I don’t know. And I don’t want to know. Does one always need a reason to love someone? I can understand that it’s not easy for you to arrive at a decision about me so fast, as you hardly know anything about me. You can take your time to decide.’

Saahil looked into Varsha’s eyes. Though she had allowed him time to think, her lovely eyes were not able to conceal the fear of rejection. He was falling for those blue eyes. He took her hands in his and said, ‘This may sound weird, but I must confess that I have fallen for you, though I hardly know anything about you.’

Two drops of tears rolled down Varsha’s cheeks, though the smile on her lips had broadened now. Saahil said, ‘I will prove myself to be a good match for you. I will do everything for you.’

# Chapter 2

Two years had passed since Saahil promised Varsha that he would do everything for her. Varsha had completed her graduation long ago and joined her elder brother's hotel business. Saahil was still jobless. Being an orphan, he hardly knew anyone who could recommend him for a job. Varsha's efforts to get him a job through her contacts had gone in vain due to his lack of experience. He could hardly meet his expenses with the money he earned from doing the project work for students.

Their love had blossomed over the two years, but stress was on the rise now. Varsha's elder brother and sole guardian, Mr. Dev, was making consistent efforts to get a perfect marriage alliance for her. This was aggravating the stress of Saahil's unemployment. One day, tired of the pressure, Varsha told Mr. Dev about Saahil. Mr. Dev didn't say a word in return. After three days, he simply said, 'Ask Saahil to have breakfast with us next Sunday.'

Owing to his unemployment, Saahil was not willing to meet Mr. Dev so soon. But after much convincing by Varsha, he agreed.

It was Sunday. Saahil got ready to meet Mr. Dev. His adrenaline level was at its peak. Vaibhav had arranged a *sherwani* for him. He slipped into the slightly oversized *sherwani* and left for Varsha's place.

Saahil didn't find it difficult to find Varsha's house, because her house was a part of one of the best hotels of the city. Mr. Dev owned the hotel. A part of it was being used by Varsha and Mr. Dev for residential purposes. The hotel was situated on a small hill, which overlooked a dense forest. The forest was intersected by an unnamed river. The whole view from the hotel was picturesque.

When Saahil reached the entrance of the house, which was separate from that of the hotel, a signboard at the gate caught his attention. It had the picture of a furious German Shepherd pouncing on a leopard. Written below was: *'The dog doesn't deal with substandard species and doesn't like those who think they are up to its standard.'* Saahil looked at himself, trying to judge his own standards.

His thought was interrupted when someone tapped on his shoulder. A person, who looked like a personal secretary, shook his hand. He was in a grey safari suit and held a handbag under his arm. He had a pair of spectacles with thick carbon frames over his eyes. His betel stained lips flashed a broad smile. Cautious not to spill even a single drop of his betel stained saliva on the ground, he said, 'Hello, myself Kashyap. I am Mr. Dev's personal secretary. He is waiting for you inside.'

Saahil's heart started racing. He was already expecting a grave, angry, possessive and strict elder brother. Saahil knew that Mr. Dev was a self-made rich businessman. People who loved him said he was full of confidence, while the people who hated him thought he was stubborn.

As he entered the house, Varsha welcomed him. To his surprise, Mr. Dev greeted him with a big smile. Mr. Dev was tall and handsome enough to give a complex to any *Bollywood* hero. Looking at Saahil in the *sherwani*, he said, 'Aha! I can already see you in the groom's attire. Good. I like optimistic people.' Saahil felt a bit relieved and wanted to thank Vaibhav for his insightfulness. But his happiness was short-lived. Soon Mr. Dev added, 'But people often fail to distinguish between optimism and overconfidence. So better be careful, because I don't like people who are overconfident.' By the time he finished the sentence, his big smile had disappeared. Saahil thought it would be safe not to jump to conclusions so fast.

After a formal breakfast, Mr. Dev came to the point without wasting any time and asked, 'Do you think you are eligible to marry Varsha?'

Saahil fumbled, but tried to sound optimistic, 'Y...Y... Yes sir, I th...think so.' Then he thought he shouldn't sound overconfident, so he added, 'But I am not sure.'

Mr. Dev rose from the sofa and said, 'So, I think we are done. You may leave now and come back when you are sure.'

Varsha made a face that all sisters make at times to blackmail their brothers emotionally, and objected, 'Bhaiya, you are being rude.'

Mr. Dev sat down on the sofa again and said, 'See Saahil, after the death of our parents, I am the only one left in this world to look after Varsha. Hence, I must be satisfied that you are eligible to marry my sister. So answer my questions. Do you have a job or do you run some business? I mean, what is the source of your income?'

This time, Saahil made sure to sound sure about everything. He said, 'I am in search of a job and I am sure I will get one very soon.'

'Hmm. Now, I already know the answers to the rest of my questions. But I will let you answer so that Varsha and you don't feel that I didn't give you a chance to prove yourself. Do you have a good balance in your bank account?'

Having a good bank balance was out of question, because Saahil didn't have a bank account at all. The only account that he had was his debt account at Chourasia's betel shop. Chourasia supplied cigarettes to him and his friends on an EMI basis without charging any interest. But Saahil had a bad reputation for maintaining a big negative balance in that account too.

In response to Mr. Dev's second question, Saahil confessed, 'I don't have a savings bank account at present.' In order to show that he was optimistic, he added, 'But I will certainly have one in future, and of course, with a huge balance in it.'

Mr. Dev looked at Varsha with a triumphant smile on his face as if he wanted to say, 'See, you have chosen a good-for-nothing.' Then he continued, 'Do you own a house?'

Saahil persevered, 'No, I don't have one at present. But I can guarantee that I will have a big one in future.' He stretched out his arms as wide as possible to show how big the house would be. He was happy that each of his answers had a hint of optimism in it.

But he was wrong. Mr. Dev looked stern and said, 'What do you think? Am I talking about getting my sister married to you, or am I giving you some bank loan on the basis of your guarantee? You don't have anything at present, but you are trying to show that you are sure about the future. By the way, how are you going to get everything in future? Do you have any plan of action in your mind?'

Saahil adhered to the prototype of his answers and said, 'I don't have one at present, but I am confident that I can form a perfect plan of action in future.'

Saahil's reply got on Mr. Dev's nerves. He yelled at Saahil. 'Are you trying to make fun of me?'

Saahil apologized for the mistake he hadn't committed and said, 'No sir. I didn't mean to.' He was telling the truth and perhaps Mr. Dev realized that.

Mr. Dev took some deep breaths in order to feel relaxed. Then he said, 'Look, it's good to be optimistic, but it's better to be a practical optimist. One can't live on optimism. One needs money to thrive in this world. And I can't let my sister marry someone who doesn't have anything except optimism. I need you to fulfil some criteria to be eligible to marry her. First criterion is that you must have a job or a business with an income of at least one lakh rupees per month.'

Saahil was clean bowled. He had heard of lakhs of rupees only in movies, in which kidnappers demanded lakhs of rupees as ransom to release the captives. At that moment, that was the only profession making lakhs in a month that he could think of. But he wondered whether Mr. Dev would like to have a kidnapper brother-in-law or not.

Mr. Dev mentioned the other criteria, 'You must own a nice house. You must possess a nice car. And don't try to fool me with a second hand car. Your bank account must have a balance of at least ten lakh rupees.' At this point, Saahil realized that Mr. Dev was really against their marriage and that's why he was deliberately setting criteria which he could never fulfil. He felt helpless. Varsha tried to intervene, but Mr. Dev asked her to keep quiet.

'Can I have some water?' Saahil somehow managed to say. He drowned the entire glass of water down his throat. Mr. Dev smiled at his condition. Why wouldn't he? After all, he was like a batsman who was facing a free hit delivery and Saahil was like the bowler. Mr. Dev had all the freedom to hit the ball anywhere and Saahil was in no position to restrict him.

Saahil and Varsha looked at each other. Varsha knew that Saahil could never fulfil the criteria mentioned by her brother. Her eyes were wet. A shadow of grief masked Saahil's face. They were seeing their dreams getting crushed right in front of their eyes.

Mr. Dev read the emotions on their faces and said, 'Don't be emotional. Emotions are like mischievous kids, and life is like a mature adult. However mischievous emotions may be, life always takes them in its stride. No emotion can change your fate, but you can if you try hard.'

Saahil mustered courage and said, 'Sir, I am an orphan. I don't have any ancestral property. I don't even have a job. How can I earn all the things that you have said? Even if I get a job, it will take me decades to fulfill all the criteria.'

'That's exactly what I am saying. I can't let my sister marry someone who doesn't have anything, neither can I keep her waiting for decades to marry you.'

Saahil's words had backfired. He didn't know what to say next. He stammered, 'But…but…but…'

'But you still want to marry her, right? Okay. Fine. Let's play a game. Try to fulfil the criteria as early as possible and I will try to get Varsha married to a suitable guy as soon as possible. The person who finishes his task first will be the winner. If you win, Varsha will be all yours. And if I win, I won't mind your presence as a guest at Varsha's wedding.'

Varsha objected, 'Bhaiya, that's unfair. Our life is not a game. Why are you doing this to us?'

'Because I care for you,' said Mr. Dev. 'But you are not bound to obey me. You people are mature enough to decide everything about your life. You can do whatever you want to. But in that case, don't expect me to be part of your happiness.'

'But, bhaiya…,' Varsha tried to object again, but Mr. Dev got to his feet, which indicated that the discussion was over. Varsha and Saahil sat speechless and looked at each other in desperation. They didn't know what to say anymore.

After a few moments of silence, Mr. Kashyap, Mr. Dev's personal secretary, walked Saahil to the gate. Saahil looked at the signboard that featured the German shepherd pouncing on the leopard, and said, 'Mr. Kashyap, this signboard can be made even better.' 'How, sir?'

'Replace the picture of the German Shepherd with that of Mr. Dev.'

# Chapter 3

Varsha and Saahil were enjoying a nice and cool evening at an inexpensive roof top garden restaurant. Saahil had decided the venue according to his budget. It had stopped raining only a few hours back. The cool breeze had a nice aroma of rain soaked earth. Saahil had already asked the waiter not to serve dinner too soon, so they could spend more time together.

After some casual conversation, Varsha asked, 'So, what do you think?'

'About what?'

'About your meeting with bhaiya. About all that he said.'

The very mention of the meeting annoyed Saahil. He said, 'It was the most horrible meeting of my life. Your brother is so irritating, ill-behaved and rude. To be very frank, he doesn't know how to behave.'

Varsha was hurt. 'How can you say that about my brother? You are so mean.'

'Oh really? I am mean? I am mean? What about your brother? What about his behavior? Wasn't that mean?'

Tension was building up. Varsha tried to justify, 'He is my brother after all. Obviously, he is worried about my future. How can you be so insensitive to call him mean?'

'I am insensitive? He is the one who is insensitive. He is the most ill mannered and insensitive brute I have ever seen.'

Varsha didn't argue anymore. She just started crying. Before Saahil could say anything, she rose from her chair and walked out, almost brushing past the waiter who was coming towards their table to serve dinner.

The waiter came to Saahil and said, 'Sir, your dinner is hot and ready.'

Saahil said, 'Thanks. But it's of no use now.' He paid the bill and left the place. His heart was heavy with a sense of guilt. He had made Varsha cry for the first time.

When Saahil reached his room, the state of his heart was evident from his face. Vaibhav said, 'You seem to be in a bad mood. What happened?'

Saahil narrated to him the entire incident that had happened between Varsha and him. Vaibhav said, 'You have committed the second most terrible crime in the world of love.'

'What is that crime?'

'Talking bad of your beloved's family members in front of her. Always praise your girlfriend's family members in front of her, even though you may not like them.'

Saahil decided to keep this in mind in future. Just out of curiosity, he asked, 'And what is the most terrible crime in the world of love?'

'Infidelity,' Vaibhav replied as a matter of fact.

Saahil spent a sleepless night pondering over the matter of their marriage, and arrived at a conclusion finally. He called Varsha the next morning, apologized to her for his behavior and asked her to meet him at the same restaurant where they had met the day before. Vaibhav advised him to take some flowers for Varsha to make her feel good. The only ones he could find on his way were garlands made out of marigold flowers, being sold in front of a temple. When he gave them to Varsha, she laughed and said, 'You are silly, but very sweet.'

Saahil was determined to praise Mr. Dev in front of Varsha this time. After they had ordered their lunch, he said, 'I am sorry for the way I talked about your brother yesterday. I shouldn't have done that. I realized that he was only doing his duty as a brother. That's why he seemed a bit rude that day. Otherwise, he is a nice person.'

'Do you really think so?'

'Of course, I do.'

'Oh. That's so sweet of you.' Looking around to check that nobody saw them, she gave him a peck on his cheek.

He said, 'I have one more thing to tell you. I thought a lot about our marriage seriously and have decided something.'

'Oh really? I knew you were capable of finding a way out. What did you decide?' Varsha asked enthusiastically.

'I think we can continue to be boyfriend and girlfriend instead of getting married. In that case, I won't have to try to fulfil any of your brother's criteria, and we can remain a couple for life, just as we are now.'

'What…? Are you out of your senses? Do you even realize that this is India? Couldn't you think of a more sensible solution than that?'

Saahil realized that things were on the verge of getting out of control again. He said, 'Wait, wait, wait. I have thought of one more solution. I am sure this one is more sensible and you will like it.'

'Yes, tell me.'

'We can marry against your brother's wishes. He may be dissatisfied initially, but he will forgive you after some days.'

'No. He won't. I know him. Why don't you find an acceptable solution instead of acting like an escapist? Why don't you think like a responsible person?' Varsha's voice radiated annoyance.

Meanwhile, the waiter arrived with the lunch and said, 'Sir, today I have brought your lunch before madam leaves without eating.'

Varsha looked at Saahil. 'See, even he has some sense of responsibility.'

Saahil felt irritated and said, 'Then why don't you marry him?'

'Fine. I will.' Varsha was in an equally aggressive mood. She addressed the waiter, 'Will you marry me?'

The waiter produced a big grin, exposing his betel-stained teeth.'Many girls want to marry me, but I am sorry, madam. I am already married and I love my Ramkali very much,' he said.

'Oh! My bad luck. Anyway, you may leave.'

The waiter left. Saahil burst into laughter. Varsha said, 'Keep on laughing, and bhaiya will get me married to someone else.'

'No. He can't. Just go on rejecting each and every alliance he gets for you. This will continue for some years, after which... you know...when your brother is no more, we'll get married.'

Varsha rose from her chair violently, scattering the served lunch all over the place, and yelled, 'You want my brother to die so we can marry? You are disgusting. You are impossible. Today, I repent falling for you. I won't meet you ever again.' She left the place.

As Varsha left, the waiter approached Saahil and asked, 'What happened, sir? Why is madam so annoyed?'

'You broke her heart by refusing to marry her. Unable to bear the grief, she went mad,' Saahil said and paid the bill.

Saahil hadn't taken Varsha's words too seriously until he realized that she was neither calling him nor receiving his calls. He even tried to meet her at her place, but she refused to meet him. A week passed. Saahil was finding it difficult to spend time without Varsha. He started roaming around their usual haunts, hoping to run into her by chance. All the places seemed gloomy to him, however. The sun at Sunset Point was upset. Love had vanished from Lovers' Point. Rose Garden seemed grief laden.

Love is such a shared experience that when one is affected, the other can't stay immune either. Varsha, in her self-imposed confinement, was trying hard to resist the temptation of communicating with Saahil. She was avoiding everything that might trigger her emotions for Saahil. She was staying away from her phone. She had stopped watching or listening to love songs. She had stopped going out of her house to avoid meeting with Saahil. She was trying hard to forget him, but memories are like the software files currently in use. Whenever you try to delete them, it prompts, 'Sorry. The action can't be completed because the memory files are open in multiple locations.'

Varsha was keeping herself busy with her brother's hotel business. One morning, she was in her bathroom, with tears rolling down her cheeks. She was brushing her teeth so hard that God only knew what she was trying to brush away – the germs from her teeth, or Saahil's thoughts from her mind. The intercom rang in the adjacent room. As Varsha received the call, a tense voice of the hotel receptionist echoed from the other side. 'Madam, I am sorry to disturb you. But we have a problem here. Can you please come to the hotel right now?'

Varsha reached the hotel in no time. 'What happened?' she asked him.

The receptionist said, 'Madam, we have a very difficult guest in room 206. We are trying our best to provide him the best of our services. But he has got complaints regarding everything. He seems determined to create problems.'

'Hmm. Let me handle him,' Varsha said and proceeded to room 206. As she pressed the doorbell, a voice answered from inside, 'Come in.'

Varsha opened the door to find the guest lounging on the sofa, his back towards her. Varsha tried to swallow her irritation and said, 'Sir, we try our best to provide all possible comforts to our guests. Is there anything that I can get for you?'

'You have already got me what I needed. I need you.' He rose from the sofa and turned towards Varsha.

'You!' Varsha cried out in surprise. All her anger sublimed. Tears started rolling down her cheeks.

'I tried to meet you so many times, but you avoided me each time. I figured this was the only way I could meet you. It took me so many days to arrange the money to book a room in your hotel.' Saahil's eyes grew wet.

'Why did you want to meet me? I thought my presence or absence in your life didn't make a difference to you. I thought you could live without me.'

'You are right. I can live without you, but it's very painful. And the thought of you living without me is even more painful.' Saahil took her in his embrace.

Varsha wanted to fight with him, scold him and blame him, but she couldn't do any of that. She just hugged him tight and cried like a child, drenching his shirt with her tears.

Saahil wiped her tears, looked into her eyes and said, 'I am sorry about what I said regarding your brother that day. I know my behavior was very immature. But now, I have realized one thing – I can't afford to lose you. I promise that I will try my best to fulfill the criteria set by Mr. Dev. I won't let anyone else marry you.'

A smile appeared on Varsha's face. She called the receptionist and said, 'The guest is not satisfied with our services. He is checking out. Please refund any advance amount taken from him.'

# Chapter 4

Saahil looked at his distorted reflection in the stainless steel statue of a Greek warrior placed outside the interviewers' chamber, and adjusted his neck tie for the umpteenth time. He was striding up and down the waiting area, fidgeting anxiously.

Tired of going through the cycle of applied-interviewed-rejected time and again, he was determined to bag this job at any cost. But he didn't know how.

He waited impatiently until the last but one candidate emerged out of the interviewers' chamber. Saahil then entered to find a lady and two gentlemen seated on revolving chairs. However, there was no chair for him.

As he greeted the interviewers, one of the gentlemen asked, 'Are you looking for a chair? Don't. You will be disappointed. You have applied for the job of a salesperson. You will have to go from door to door to sell the product. You won't be offered a chair in most houses. In fact, people might not even let you enter their houses. So let's have the interview in a practical scenario.'

'I understand, sir,' Saahil said and started showing his certificates to them.

The other gentleman, who was in a white suit, said, 'The vendors at the vegetable market are very good salespersons though they may not possess any certificates. We don't need your certificates. We just need your skill and experience. Tell us about your experience in the sales field.'

Saahil hesitated, 'Sir, I don't have any experience.'

'Why should we hire you then?' asked the gentleman.

Saahil almost pleaded, 'Sir, I desperately need the job.'

'But your desperation is of no use to us. We want experience. You may leave.' The gentleman's voice was harsh.

Saahil uttered a formal 'thank you', and left with a failure-stricken face.

After he had left, the gentleman said, 'There is no place for inexperienced people in our company.'

The lady interviewer said, 'But the boy is desperate for the job. And one who needs a job desperately often works more sincerely. So, let's hire desperation instead of experience this time.'

That evening, Saahil and Varsha were strolling by the river. After the long hectic day of giving interviews, the cool breeze by the river and Varsha's proximity felt very soothing to Saahil. However, Varsha was unusually silent.

Saahil asked, 'What's the matter?'

'I am feeling hopeless. Bhaiya is trying his best to get a suitable alliance for me. I am afraid. I can live without you, but I can't live with anyone other than you.'

Saahil's cell rang that very moment. After talking for two minutes, he cut the line, looked at Varsha, and said, 'I hadn't thought the company would offer me the job, but they took the decision quite quickly. I got the job.'

Varsha stood startled for a moment. Then she yelled, 'You got the job?'

'I got the job.'

'You mean a real job - a job with duties and a salary?'

'That's what a job consists of, I suppose. Yes. I got a real job – a job with duties and a salary.'

'Wow. Wow. That's just so amazing.' Varsha jumped with excitement, but Saahil didn't seem equally excited.

Varsha asked, 'Aren't you happy?'

'I am happy. But I wonder whether I will be able to fulfill the conditions set by Mr. Dev with my petty salary.'

'Don't get disheartened. Everything will be alright. At least we took our first step toward fulfilling our dreams,' Varsha said and embraced him.

The following morning, Saahil's cell rang at seven. As he received the call, a lady on the other side said, 'Reach the office at eight. Your training starts today.'

Saahil looked at the wall clock lazily.

'Hello?' asked the lady.

'Yes, madam. I will be there in time.'

'Good.'She cut the line.

Saahil reached the office on time and found seven other new appointees waiting inside the conference room where their training was supposed to start. A peculiar thing caught his attention. There were pictures of dartboards everywhere – on the walls, the ceiling, the door, the training kits, even on the furniture.

The lady who had been one of the interviewers the day before, entered the room. She seemed to be in her mid-forties. She started, 'Good morning, everyone. I am Mrs. Bandana Das. I'll ask you all one question. What do you see around you?'

No one uttered a word, but looked around cluelessly.

She repeated the question. This time, one of the appointees replied, 'Dartboards.'

'Yes! And what do they signify?'

Again, everyone gained a blank look on their faces.

Mrs. Bandana said, 'Target, boys and girls, target. A salesperson's dictionary has only one word – target. His career, his life, his success – everything revolves around only one word – target. Look around you. You are surrounded by targets. Look at the ceiling. The sharp swords of targets are hanging over your heads. Look below. You are sitting on volcanoes of targets.'

A few appointees rose from their chairs to appraise the metaphorical volcanoes they were sitting on and found pictures of dartboards on their chairs.

Mrs. Bandana continued, 'The motive behind these omnipresent dartboards is to not let you forget the sole aim of your life – to achieve your monthly targets.'

After three days of rigorous training, Mrs. Bandana said, 'Come on, my brave boys and girls. You are now all set to proceed on your journey to conquer the kingdom of customers. Remember two things. First – customer is king. Second – you must conquer the king. And here are your weapons.' She handed each of the new appointees a bag full of slimming kits and asked them to disperse.

Saahil formed his own strategy for reaching out to customers who were more likely to buy the slimming kits. He contacted a friend who worked as a gym instructor and gathered information about the overweight people attending the gym. He also made a list of people whom Varsha, Vaibhav and he knew personally. He decided to make visits to the more affluent areas of the city, since people there had extravagant lifestyles and were generous eaters.

The first visit of Saahil's career turned out to be a disaster. The customer was an insolent lady with an I-know-everything attitude. As it was Saahil's first-ever visit in the field, he was a bit nervous. He stammered, 'Madam, this kit…I mean, the slimming kit…the kit, you know…'

The lady snatched the kit from his hands and spoke fluently, 'Sir, this slimming kit promises a reduction of at least five kgs of weight in less than a month. The kit contains a slimming belt that you can use on specific parts of your body to lose inches miraculously. The kit also contains two packets of green tea and two bottles of slimming oil. Over and above all this, you get the user guide absolutely free. The actual market price of the kit is five thousand rupees. But as a promotional offer from the company, you are getting the kit at an unbelievable price of only two thousand, nine hundred and ninety nine rupees.'

Saahil stared at her gape-mouthed.

The lady added, 'This is how you sell your product to a customer. The number of salespersons I have met is more than the number of customers you have tried selling it to. Now, get lost with your slimming kit.'

The rest of the customers were not that rude. One of the customers was quite well-behaved and even offered Saahil a chair and a glass of soft drink. He was a patient listener. He discussed all the aspects of the slimming kit with him for half an hour. Saahil felt confident that he would buy the product from him.

However, he politely refused and said, 'Actually, I am writing an article on slimming kits. Thanks a lot for giving me all the information I needed.'

Saahil didn't know that even polite persons could be so cunning. Some customers were innocent enough to ask, 'Can I have a free trial period of three months before buying one?' or 'Will I get my money back if I am not satisfied with the results after using the product for two months?' Saahil wondered how much of the slimming oil and green tea would remain after a trial period of two or three months.

Overenthusiastic customers were not uncommon either. Every day, some plump girl would call and thank Saahil for every nano-inch of reduction in the girth of her waist. Finally, one day, Saahil had to change his contact number when the girl asked, 'Now that I have lost one hundred grams in last three weeks, do you think ours will be a nice pair to look at?'

Saahil gradually learned to nod and smile at everything that customers said.

He nodded and smiled when an optimist said, 'No way. I believe only in winning. I won't lose anything, not even weight.'

He nodded and smiled when someone freaked out, 'Sinners! You are all sinners. You all are cold blooded murderers. Every entity in this world has life. Even the fat cells of our body have life. And you are asking people to kill those innocent little fat cells! Cruel! Very cruel! You won't be forgiven for your sins.'

In spite of all his disastrous adventures, Saahil managed to get at least some unsuspecting customers who didn't mind paying a few thousand bucks to get rid of a few inches. Whenever he felt low, two things kept him going– Varsha's love and the dartboards.

At the end of the month, Mrs. Bandana called him to her chamber, handed him an envelope and said, 'Your first salary. I am giving it to you personally because you are the only boy who has achieved the monthly target. Good job. Now, answer my question. Can the word *success* do without that extra *s* at its end?'

Saahil stood confused and wordless.

Mrs. Bandana continued, 'No. It can't do without that extra *s* at the end. It is significant of the fact that success never comes to one in an isolated way. It always brings with it happiness, money, fame and much more. Remember this whenever you feel tired or disappointed while working. You will feel energized again.'

# Chapter 5

'I had wanted to celebrate the occasion at a good restaurant. Why did you insist on celebrating by having *pav bhaji* from some street vendor? The *pav bhaji* was delicious though,' Saahil said.

'The celebration was for your first salary, and I can't let your hard-earned money drain into costly restaurants. We should save money so we can shape our future.' Varsha handed Saahil the ten-rupee coin that the *pav bhaji* vendor had returned as change.

Looking at the coin, Saahil smiled cynically and said, 'The shape of our future is exactly the same as that of the coin – a big zero.'

Varsha held Saahil's hand and asked, 'Can we go on a long drive?'

Saahil nodded and they got on his bicycle.

Varsha started talking, 'You are doing your best. You shouldn't feel depressed. You should think positive. You should…'

'I should do this. I should do that. I should…I should…I should…I know all that I should do. I am trying to abide by all the "should"s. But the problem is that life doesn't abide by any of them. It just goes on its own way. I work day and night. I don't even get time to spend with you. The constant pressure to achieve my monthly targets has eaten my life up. I am afraid to look at calendars these days. Even my watch looks like a dartboard to me. I digest all the harsh words from ill-behaved customers without complaining, and what do I get at the end of the month? Just ten thousand rupees. That's when my heart aches. How much will I be able to save for our future with such a meagre salary? It will take me decades to fulfill the criteria set by Mr. Dev.'

Saahil stopped the bicycle. Varsha got down and wrapped her arms around Saahil. 'Don't worry about anything. Everything is going to be alright. Our love is true. We won't fail.'

'You know, Mr. Dev is correct about one thing at least. It's good to be optimistic, but it's better to be a practical optimist. Now, let's go.'

Saahil dropped Varsha near her house and returned to his room to find a few old friends waiting for him. Vaibhav said, 'You look quite stressed out these days. I thought a small party might change your mood.'

Saahil felt happy. 'Thanks, buddy. You are a real friend. I have been working like a machine for the last one month. I need this party badly to feel that I am still human.'

There is nothing more relaxing than a fun-filled time spent with friends. The party continued till late into the night. By two o'clock, all were spent and asleep except Saahil and Vaibhav.

Vaibhav licked off the last drop of beer from his glass and said, 'Life is like alcohol. You can't stop loving it no matter how much you dislike it. So, it's better to love it.'

'Everyone becomes a philosopher after taking a few pegs of alcohol. I am in no mood to listen to your philosophies.'

'I am not philosophizing. I am not drunk.'

'Everyone says "I am not drunk" after taking a few pegs.'

'But everyone doesn't try to solve your problems after taking a few pegs. What's the matter? Why are you tense?'

Saahil sighed, 'I can't lose Varsha at any cost. Nor can I fulfill Mr. Dev's criteria with my small salary.'

'Then quit the job and try something else.'

'It's not that easy. I am afraid to leave the job. There is no guarantee that I will make more money if I try something else.'

'Do you think all successful people in the world had guarantee cards in their hands before they ventured on journeys that were full of risks and uncertainties? Despite the fifty other candidates there, you got the job. Why? Because you were determined. You were the only salesperson to have achieved the monthly target. Why? Because you were determined. I am sure you won't fail if you are determined to earn more by some other means.'

Saahil looked at Vaibhav with his eyes wide open and said, 'You are right. You are absolutely right. I should quit the job and try to do something else.'

When Saahil told Varsha about his decision, she didn't seem very happy. However, she said, 'Though I don't think this is a wise decision, I am with you in whatever you do. Anyway, what will you do if you quit the job?'

'I will still be a salesperson, but I will work for myself, not for others.'

'Do whatever you want to do. Just don't let anyone else marry me.'

'I won't. I promise.'

'But it won't be easy for you to resign. As per the norms of the company, you will have to give a three months' notice before resigning.'

'I know one hundred and one ways to get myself kicked out of the job. I won't resign. They will kick me out with all due respect.'

'Oh, I see. So you are going to create nuisance so that the company will kick you out?'

'You are smart.'

'You are going to cheat the company that gave you your first job and first salary.'

'This can't be called cheating. We can give it a better name like…like…"utilization of opportunity".'

'But the meaning remains the same – cheating. I am sure there must be a better and genuine way to handle things.'

Saahil thought for a while and said, 'Alright. I will try to find a better way because I don't like to do something that you don't like.' Saahil's words brought a big smile to Varsha's face.

It took Saahil two days to find a 'better and genuine' way. On the third day, he met Mrs. Bandana in her chamber. She was busy with some files kept on her table, the top of which was again a dartboard design. She tossed a bunch of waste papers into the dustbin, the lid of which also had a picture of a dartboard. She then offered Saahil a chair. 'What happened? Any good news? Be careful. I don't like to hear bad news at the beginning of the day.' She knew from her experience that an employee entering her chamber without a smile on his face always brought bad news.

Her words aggravated Saahil's tension. He thought that it would have been better perhaps had he met her in the evening to give her the bad news. However, he gathered his courage and asked, 'Madam, what if someone wants to resign at once without giving three months' notice?'

'Don't even think of it. The company is very clear and strict regarding its policies. I repeat - clear and strrrict!'

'But madam, I need to resign at once. This is a matter of life and death for me.'

'My eardrums are semipermeable. They do not permit idioms and movie dialogues. Say something genuine and believable.' Contrary to Saahil's fear, Mrs. Bandana didn't get angry.

'Madam, what if I give one month's notice instead of three months. I will work for that month without taking any salary or incentive, and I promise to achieve my target for that month without fail. However, I will decide my own working hours, and once I achieve my target for the month, the company will accept my resignation at once and I won't be an employee of the company anymore.'

Mrs. Bandana put down her pen and said, 'Hmm. Now that sounds interesting. Alright. Meet me tomorrow.'

She called Saahil to her chamber the following day and said, 'The company has agreed to your proposal. But are you sure you are doing the right thing? I mean, leaving a promising career just like that?'

'Promising? Promising for me or for the company?' Saahil smiled.

Mrs. Bandana smiled too – it was less of a smile, and more of an unspoken acknowledgement.

Saahil proceeded to work on his plan at once. He borrowed some money from Vaibhav and Mr. Das, the librarian. As Saahil's monthly target was to sell thirty slimming kits, he purchased thirty of them from the company with the money he had borrowed. Then, he met Mrs. Bandana and said, 'I sold the thirty slimming kits to myself. As per my promise, I have achieved my monthly target. Now, the company should keep its promise and accept my resignation.'

The company kept its promise. Saahil's resignation was accepted at once. Mrs. Bandana said, 'Saahil, I don't know what you are up to, but I hope you succeed in whatever you do. I like sincere people like you. My good wishes are always with you. If you ever need my help, don't hesitate to ask for it.'

Saahil thanked Mrs. Bandana again before setting off to sell the thirty slimming kits he had purchased from the company. He worked day and night. Owing to his sincere efforts and past experience, he was able to sell all the kits within twenty days. He sold the kits at a price marginally higher than his purchase price. In the end, he made a profit of fifteen thousand rupees after repaying the money he had borrowed from Vaibhav and Mr. Das.

The amount of this profit was more than his monthly salary.

He called Varsha up and said, 'You are right. There is always a better and genuine way of doing everything. I made a profit of fifteen thousand rupees, and I didn't even lose the goodwill of the people at the company. I owe all this to you. Now, this calls for a celebration, but not at some *pav bhaji* vendor's stall. Let's go to a nice restaurant.'

'As you wish, my prince charming.' Varsha showered kisses on Saahil through her cell phone.

# Chapter 6

*I have news for you. Come to my place. Dev.*

Saahil's hands trembled and he dropped his cell phone to the floor. An SMS directly from Mr. Dev was a new and unexpected turn for him.

When Saahil reached Mr. Dev's place that day, he greeted him and offered him to sit. He didn't quite like the smile on Mr. Dev's face, though. His sixth sense warned him that something adverse was going to be revealed to him. Varsha was tense too.

'I have finalized on an alliance for Varsha,' Mr. Dev declared with the sternness of a dictator in his voice.

'What? How could you? You should have asked me at least,' Varsha objected.

'I went on arranging alliances, and you went on rejecting them so you could buy time to let Saahil prove himself. This time, I didn't want to take a chance.'

Varsha looked at Saahil. 'Why are you sitting quietly? Don't you have anything to say about the matter?'

Saahil stammered, 'Yes. Of course. I want to say…I mean…I want to ask…' He looked at Mr. Dev. 'Sir, may I ask who the lucky man is?' he asked politely.

Varsha shouted, 'Nice. Very nice. So that's all you have to say? You don't have a problem with the marriage? The only thing that you want to know is who the *lucky man* is?'

'No. I mean...' Saahil struggled for words.

'No. No. Go on. Ask some more stupid questions. Ask about his appearance, education and profession. Ask when and where the wedding will be held?' Varsha shouted again.

Mr. Dev laughed loudly, reminding Saahil of some of the most villainous demons he had seen in mythological movies. Then he said, 'I think it's your right to know everything about him. His name is Alok. He has got so much ancestral property that he didn't need an education or involvement in a profession. He earns lakhs of rupees from just his property, sitting at home.'

Varsha said, 'Wait a minute. So you want me to marry an uneducated, unemployed, idle donkey who doesn't have anything of his own? His property, his money – everything belongs to his ancestors. Saahil is much better than him. At least, he is educated, and whatever he earns is the result of his own effort.'

'So what? Saahil can never earn as much as Alok does. Anyway, I didn't call you two here to argue with you. I just wanted you to know that I have successfully cleared the first hurdle of my game against Saahil. I am letting you know all this now because I don't want to be blamed later of not playing fair.'

Varsha argued, 'Bhaiya, I have told you before that our lives are not a game...'

Mr. Dev waved off any further arguments and left.

After a brief moment of silence, Varsha looked at Saahil who was nibbling on a *gulab jamun* that had been offered to them by Mr. Dev on the occasion of the settlement of the marriage alliance, and asked, 'What do you think?'

'A bit hard on the outside, but soft on the inside,' Saahil gave her his valuable opinion.

Varsha appeared thoughtful. 'I hope your opinion about bhaiya is correct. But what if he turns out to be hard on the inside too?'

'Bhaiya? Who is talking about bhaiya? I am talking about the *gulab jamuns*.'

'You are impossible,' Varsha yelled.

Saahil was not as relaxed as he was trying to put out. When he left Varsha's place with a tense mind, it started to drizzle. The roads of the city were almost deserted. The street lights were struggling to rescue the city from the darkness that had engulfed it. Saahil's old and rusted bicycle tore through the silence of the moment. As he wandered around the city aimlessly, the deserted roads aggravated his sense of loneliness. He was able to imagine how his Varsha-less life could be.

When his calf muscles rebelled after two hours of continuous pedalling in the rain, he returned to his room. He was drenched from head to toe and was shivering with the cold. Vaibhav looked at him and asked, 'I am going to make coffee. Would you like a cup of hot and strong coffee?'

'Yes, I need it badly,' Saahil said as he changed out of his wet clothes. He wrapped a shawl around himself and squatted near the electric cooking heater on which Vaibhav was preparing coffee.

Vaibhav served him his cup and asked, 'You look devastated. What's the problem?'

'A hopeful girlfriend and a hopeless would-be brother-in-law. As such, it's not easy for me to fulfill the criteria set by Mr. Dev. In addition, he is trying to make things more difficult for me by expediting the preparations for Varsha's wedding,' Saahil said and sipped the steaming coffee from his cup. He told Vaibhav everything that had happened at Varsha's place that day.

In order to console him, Vaibhav said, 'Let's go to Chaurasia's betel shop. You will feel better.'

'He must have shut his shop by now.'

'No, he must be waiting for me. We have a very important matter to discuss.'

'What matter?'

'Foreign Policy of India.'

'Are you joking?'

'No. I am not.'

'You are going to discuss India's foreign policy with Chaurasia, the man for whom *foreign* stands for the nearest neighbouring city that's a hundred kilometers away, and *policy* just means a life insurance policy? What are you going to gain by discussing it with him? Do *you* even have anything to do with India's foreign policy?'

'Not everything is done with the intention of gaining something. Some things are carried out just for the sake of knowledge,' Vaibhav replied very coolly.

'I don't understand how you handle so much knowledge,' Saahil said sarcastically and accompanied Vaibhav to Chaurasia's betel shop.

Chaurasia handed Vaibhav a *Churasia's special paan*. Vaibhav chewed on it and marvelled, 'Wow! Yours are the best *paans* I have ever had – just magical. How do you prepare such magical *paans*?' Vaibhav flattered Chaurasia like this sometimes in order to ensure that his credit account with him ran smoothly.

Truly flattered by Vaibhav's words, Chaurasia grinned, baring his betel stained teeth and said, 'There is no magic. I just try to make my customers happy. The *paans* become magical on their own.'

Vaibhav thought for a moment, then addressed Saahil. 'You told me that you would work as a freelance salesperson after quitting your job at the slimming kit company. I think you should start your office as soon as possible, instead of wasting your time getting depressed. Like Chaurasia, try to make your clients happy by providing them your best services. Let's see what happens.'

'Hmm. Perhaps, you are right,' Saahil said. A shadow of depression still lingered over his face.

# Chapter 7

*We provide anything your heart desires*

Saahil looked at the caption written on the signboard of his new office, and it produced a smile of satisfaction on his face. Finally, he had managed to start his own office, though any person in his right mind would not call it an office. It was a large log cabin which had been used as a grocery shop once upon a time. Saahil had got its walls painted with the cheapest paint he could get in the market. The roof had already been repaired many times, thus not leaving any need or scope for further repairs.

An age-old banyan tree stood adjacent to the cabin. The weirdest thing about the tree-cabin duo was a lean branch from the banyan tree that had gained authorized access into the cabin through a small hole in one of its walls. The access had been authorized by Mr. Ashok, the owner of the cabin. He had agreed to rent out the cabin to Saahil on the condition that Saahil would never chop off the branch fully. He was allowed occasional trimming though. After looking around and feeling assured that he was not being watched, he had whispered the reason into Saahil's ear, 'There lives a righteous and helpful ghost in the banyan tree, and he rests his tail on this particular branch. If you cut it, you will certainly injure his tail and unleash his wrath. In that case, he will forget his good nature and create havoc. I can't let that happen. For years, he has been protecting this cabin and my house which is adjacent to the cabin. By the way, are you not afraid to work here in the presence of a ghost?'

'No. I am not. I live with a creature who is weirder than ghosts.'

'Who?'

'My roommate, Vaibhav. By the way, how do you know that the ghost has a tail? I mean, humans do not have tails. So how did the ghost develop a tail after his death?'

'Oh! You are so ignorant about ghosts! You see, we humans have legs for walking and maintaining balance, but a ghost does not have legs. As a compensatory mechanism, thus, he develops a tail for moving and maintaining balance.'

'Oh, I see! That's so scientific!' Saahil had admired. 'But how do you know all this?'

'It's very simple. Haven't you seen pictures of ghosts in story books and magazines? Have you ever seen one who has got legs?'

'No, never. I must be ashamed of my ignorance about ghosts. The knowledge you possess about ghosts is really appreciable and the sources of your knowledge are so authentic.'

Mr. Ashok had smiled boastfully.

Saahil had decided that if someone were to ask him about the branch, he would simply explain that the whole arrangement was designed by an interior decorator friend, and that it served the dual purpose of style and an eco-friendly environment inside the office.

'Nice signboard! Now stop admiring it. Let's go inside,' said Varsha, dragging Saahil out of his thoughts and into the cabin.

The furniture inside consisted only of a table, two chairs and a cupboard. Some basic stationery and a second-hand computer were placed on the table. A second-hand pedestal fan stood in one corner of the office. The fan was semi-automatic – after switching on the power supply, the blades had to be provided an initial rotational force manually with the help of a pen inserted through the safety grills to make the blades move.

A small inauguration ceremony was conducted in the presence of six to seven people, including Varsha and Saahil. Everything was according to Saahil's budget - a budget office, budget furniture, and budget guests. The only thing in plenitude was the genuine well-wishes of the guests.

Addressing the guests, Saahil said, 'This office is concerned with sales and purchases. If you know anyone who wants to sell or buy something, send him to me. I am going to deal in everything, from household goods to vehicles, both old and new. I am going to help buyers reach sellers and vice versa, and earn my commission on each successful deal. I need all your support.'

After all the guests left, Varsha held Saahil's hand and said, 'I have got something very important to tell you. Bhaiya had asked our family priest to suggest a suitable date for my wedding. According to the priest, the most auspicious date for it is exactly seven months from now. I don't know whether this is good or bad news. I don't know whether I should be happy that we have got at least seven months' time in hand, or worried that it might be too less.'

'Varsha, the only thing I know is that I am not going to let anyone else marry you.'

Varsha embraced Saahil. 'I believe you,' she whispered.

Saahil realized that he didn't have much time left in hand. He started working day and night. In the daytime, he would travel door to door on his bicycle and ask the inhabitants of each house if they wanted to buy or sell something. He kept records of all the data he collected and promised to get back to them as soon as he found buyers or sellers that suited their requests. He never forgot to leave with them his business card that contained his cell number and office address. Each evening, he returned to his office and entered all the data that he had collected that day into his computer, so that it would be easy for him to search for items that people wanted to buy or sell. He also attended to clients visiting his office during this time.

Whenever he found a buyer for a particular item available, he arranged a meeting between the buyer and the seller. He presided over the meeting personally, took care of the transaction, and made sure that the exchange was successfully accomplished. Even after the finalization of a deal, he helped his clients complete the official formalities involved in the transaction, and made sure that the buyer got the item and the seller got his money without hassle. Only then did he accept his commission from his clients. Though his sincerity made the job hectic for him, he rapidly gained popularity as a good salesperson. The basic lessons of salesmanship that he had learned during his tenure at the slimming kit company served as the backbone of his success.

Working day and night, Saahil managed to get a large number of clients within a span of two months. Some people became his regular clients, owing to his responsible behavior and sincerity, and he didn't need to go from door to door to get clients anymore. He started spending most of his time at his office now. The only time he went out was during the finalization and processing of deals. He started earning a good amount of money too, but it was still not enough to fulfil the criteria set by Mr. Dev. He needed to earn more.

Mr. Ashok, owner of the cabin, attributed Saahil's success to the helpful ghost living in the banyan tree. He would occasionally come to Saahil's office to check that the branch and the ghost's tail were intact.

One evening, Mr. Ashok dropped in on Saahil unexpectedly. It was raining heavily that day and the weather had turned quite cold. Saahil had no clients to attend to for the same reason. Mr. Ashok settled his wet umbrella and shoes outside, and entered the office with a thermos in his hand. 'I thought you must be feeling cold, so I brought some tea. Let's have it together. I hope I am not disturbing you.'

'Of course not. It's nice that you came. I don't have much on my agenda today anyway. Thanks for the tea. I really needed it.'

Sipping tea from his cup, Mr. Ashok started, 'I am happy that my cabin has been rented out again. After the grocer left, it remained unoccupied for months. Nobody wanted to rent a haunted cabin, and I didn't want to cheat anyone by hiding the fact about the ghost. You agreed to rent the cabin despite the ghost. Thank you.'

'Why did the grocer leave this place?'

'I have told you already that the ghost is a righteous one. He didn't like the grocer adulterating things. I advised him many times to refrain from adding other substances to the food items as the ghost wouldn't tolerate it, but he didn't listen to me and went on mixing things. One morning, when he opened the shop, he found things oddly mixed with each other – flour mixed with mustard oil, rice mixed with kerosene, sugar mixed with chilli powder and so on. He suffered a huge loss, so he shut down the business and left.'

'Who did all this mixing?'

'Who do you think? The ghost, obviously. But you need not worry. The ghost likes you since you are a sincere boy and you don't cheat people.'

Though Saahil didn't believe in the ghost story, he preferred not to hurt Mr. Ashok's sentiments regarding the ghost, and didn't probe any further. As such, the only thing that he was bothered about at that moment was how to expand his business. Steering the conversation away from the ghost, he said, 'I have got very less time in hand and need to earn a lot more money. I don't know what to do.'

Mr. Ashok looked thoughtful for a moment. 'I am not an expert in business," he started, "but I think you are focusing on less important clients and are ignoring the more important ones.'

'I don't get you.'

'You are only focusing on common folk who occasionally want to sell something, but are ignoring business establishments like car dealers, real estate developers, furniture dealers, etc. The sole purpose of these establishments is to sell their products. If you work for them on a commission, you will earn more. However, you should do that without ignoring your current clients.'

'Wow! Excellent idea. Who said you are not an expert in business?' Saahil exclaimed, then added after a pause, 'But they already have their own salespersons. Why will they hire me?'

'That's for you to figure out.' Mr. Ashok thought for a while, then added, 'Although, we have got someone who can help you solve this problem.' He further asked Saahil to hold the banyan tree's branch hanging inside the office.

Without questioning, Saahil grasped it.

Mr. Ashok warned, 'Be gentle. You will hurt him.'

'Hurt whom?' Saahil looked puzzled, and loosened his grip slightly.

'The ghost. You are holding his tail,' Mr. Ashok said plainly.

For a moment, Saahil felt uneasy at the thought of holding a ghost's tail, and was about to pull his hand off. But the very next moment, he smiled at his own folly and decided to let the drama continue.

Mr. Ashok continued, 'Now, repeat what I say - Oh, respected helpful ghost!'

Saahil repeated, 'Oh, respected helpful ghost.'

'I am helpless and at your mercy,' Mr. Ashok said.

Saahil repeated, 'I am helpless and at your mercy.'

'Please help me fight my financial problems and guide me in my journey to find a solution.'

'Please help me fight my financial problems and guide me in my journey to find the solutions.' Saahil suppressed his laughter with much difficulty as he finished the sentence.

# Chapter 8

Saahil found himself at the car showroom, getting bored while waiting in the lobby. He hadn't witnessed a single customer entering the showroom since he came. It had been two hours and the sales manager hadn't spared the time to meet him yet.

When an employee of the car showroom told Saahil that the sales manager's name was Mr. Bijli, he couldn't suppress his laughter. *Bijli*, which meant thunder, was a popular name for girls. He had never met a man named Bijli. Mr. Bijli, a man in his forties, left no chance to shout at his subordinates for some reason or the other. His thunderous voice justified his name.

Saahil noticed the tag-line written in plastic letters on the wall behind the receptionist. Meant for their customers, it was supposed to read *'We grow with you'*, but somehow the letters of 'with' had gone missing due to some damage, and it only read '*We grow … you.*'

Mr. Bijli shouted at the receptionist, 'Do you grow your customers now? Are they trees? Come on, show me how you grow the customers. When a customer visits us next time, you must grow his height by a foot. I want to see how you do it. If you fail to do so, you will be fired.'

The receptionist struggled to say something, but the drizzle of his words was overpowered by Mr. Bijli's thunderous shouting.

Mr. Bijli then noticed the sweeper who was cleaning the glass door of the showroom. In order to remove some stubborn stain from it, he was rubbing the brush hard over one part, not realizing that he was making fresh scratches on the glass in the process. This infuriated Mr. Bijli even more. He shouted at the sweeper, 'What the hell are you doing? Who asked you to rub the glass so hard? It's costly glass. But it's of no use telling you. You don't have a brain. You have only got dirt in your head. Clean that dirt first.'

Two salespersons who were smiling at the whole situation became Mr. Bijli's next target. He shouted at them, 'What are you smiling at? You are no different than him. If you people had any brains, it would have reflected in your monthly sales reports.'

Tired of his shouting-spree and unable to find a new victim, Mr. Bijli returned to his cabin. Growing impatient, Saahil followed Mr. Bijli into his cabin. He greeted him with utmost decency. 'Good afternoon, Mr. Bijli. Could you please spare just five minutes of your valuable time for me?'

But Mr. Bijli behaved in the most unexpected manner. He shouted at Saahil, 'Get out of here. How dare you call me Mr. Bijli?'

'Oh. Sorry, sir. I should have addressed you as "sir" instead of calling you by your name,' Saahil apologized.

Mr. Bijli got even more furious. 'You need not address me as "sir". You may call me Mr. Iyer. How dare you make fun of me by calling me Mr. Bijli!'

'I am sorry, Mr. Iyer. I didn't know that you didn't prefer being addressed by your first name.'

'Who told you that my name is Bijli?'

'One of the employees of your showroom.'

Mr. Iyer tried to control his anger. 'Oh, I see. It's not your fault then. All the employees here are good for nothing. They can't do anything sensible, but indulge in stupid name-calling. My voice may sound like thunder to them, but I don't care. These morons only understand such tone and language.' Mr. Iyer gulped down some water from his glass and continued, 'Anyway, what can I do for you?'

Saahil handed him his business card and introduced himself. Mr. Iyer glanced at the card and said, 'So you are a freelance salesperson. If I am not mistaken, you want to work for us on commission basis, right?'

'Yes.'

'But we already have our own salespersons. Why should we hire you – give me three reasons.'

'First, your showroom has not sold a single car in the last fifteen days. Second, your showroom has witnessed a reduction of forty percent in sales in the last six months. Third, you are not going to lose anything by hiring me. I will take my commission only if I am able to make sales.'

'Don't try to impress me with your homework. That's a very old tactic. Say something more promising.'

Saahil rose from his chair. 'I would rather do something more promising. I only need a promise from you on behalf of your staff that my clients will not be harassed or cheated by any means, and they won't be charged extra on account of my commission. The company will pay me my commission from its profit.'

The confidence in Saahil's voice moved Mr. Iyer. He simply said, 'Done!' After Saahil left, it took him some time to believe that he had actually agreed to Saahil's proposal. He murmured, 'He was not bragging, I hope.'

Over the next three days, Saahil did a good deal of research on the internet about the cars that Mr. Iyer's showroom had sold. He befriended a salesperson from the showroom and gained some more knowledge about the cars there.

He then approached his existing clients who wanted to sell their old cars and buy new ones. One such client was Mr. Naresh. Due to his faith in Saahil, he wanted Saahil to help him with buying a new car.

Saahil took him to Mr. Iyer's showroom. One of the salespersons attended them, but most of the work of a salesperson was done by Saahil. 'Sir, which car are you planning to buy?' he asked Mr. Naresh.

'Though I have the budget of a sedan, I would like to buy a hatchback as I don't like to show off.'

'You are so humble, sir,' said Saahil. 'Would you like to buy the petrol variant or the diesel variant?'

'Though a difference of one or two lakh rupees is not a big deal for me, I would like to buy the petrol variant.

People may say that I am showing off if I buy the costlier diesel variant. And I don't like to show off, you know?'

'I must salute you for your modesty, sir,' Saahil praised.

Mr. Naresh smiled gracefully.

Saahil asked again, 'Sir, would you like to purchase the car on EMI or pay the whole amount in a lump sum?'

'Do you think I don't have enough money to pay the price in a lump sum?'

'Not at all, sir. I would never dare to think so.'

Mr. Naresh continued, 'I have got enough money to buy this whole showroom along with all the cars in it. I still want to purchase the car on EMI since paying the whole amount in a lump sum may make people think that I am a show-off. And you know...'

'You don't like to show off, sir,' Saahil completed the sentence for him.

'Correct. How did you know?'

'Your down-to-earth personality speaks for itself, sir,' said Saahil with folded hands.

Mr. Naresh smiled and proceeded to check out the cars on display. The salesperson accompanying them turned to Saahil and whispered, 'Don't you feel irritated while dealing with such annoying customers?'

'Yes, I do, but I try to digest it in the hope of getting the item sold.'

Based on his research, Mr. Naresh had developed a liking for a particular model before coming to the showroom. After checking out that model, he decided to go for it and paid an advance. Saahil was more than happy, and so was Mr. Iyer.

It was not uncommon for Saahil to get difficult clients. Mr. Sharma, who was a tech-savvy person, knew more about cars than any salesperson did. When Saahil took him to the showroom, he checked out all the models available there and concluded that none of them had been designed perfectly. He asked Mr. Iyer for a pen and a piece of paper. With the help of various indecipherable diagrams and sketches, he explained to Mr. Iyer how an ideal car should be designed. After the thirty minutes' session, he said, 'I hope I have made you understand how exactly my car should be. When can I expect my perfect car to be delivered to me?'

Mr. Iyer looked at Saahil helplessly and addressed Mr. Sharma, 'Sir, I hope you understand that we just sell cars. We don't design or manufacture them, so it won't be possible on our part to design and manufacture a customised car just for you. I request you to choose one from the cars that are already available in our showroom.'

'You didn't get me. I want you to contact the manufacturing unit of the car company and tell them to get my car manufactured according to the specifications I have mentioned to you.'

'Sir, I am afraid that it won't be possible for the company to manufacture a single car of a particular type.'

Mr. Sharma seemed disappointed. 'On the other hand, I think you are not prepared to take the extra burden.'

Saahil felt the tension building up and intervened, 'Mr. Sharma, please let me handle this. Mr. Iyer is a very efficient person. I am sure he will find a solution. Let me talk to him. In the mean time, why don't you enjoy a cup of coffee in the lobby?'

After Mr. Sharma had gone to the lobby, Mr. Iyer turned to Saahil and said, 'Is he out of his mind? Tell him to choose a car from the cars available here, otherwise he may leave.'

'Relax, Mr. Iyer! Look, Mr. Sharma is watching us through the glass wall of your cabin, but I am sure he can't hear us. Now, take out your phone and act as if you are talking to someone.'

Mr. Iyer did exactly as Saahil had asked him to do. After fifteen minutes of this charade, Saahil went into the lobby and congratulated Mr. Sharma. 'Mr. Sharma, Mr. Iyer has solved your problem. The company is ready to manufacture the car according to the specifications mentioned by you.'

Excited, Mr. Sharma rose from the sofa at once. 'Wow! That's really nice. I must thank Mr. Iyer.'

Saahil said, 'But there is a small problem. As the company will have to manufacture a customised model for you, the production cost will be very high. The car will cost you about five to six times more than the usual cost.'

Mr. Sharma almost fell back on the cozy sofa in the lobby. He could just utter, 'Oh!' After a pause of two minutes, he said, 'I think even these cars in the showroom are not that bad after all. I can choose one of them.'

'No, Mr. Sharma. There is no need to compromise. The company is ready to manufacture the car of your choice.'

'No, no, Saahil. One should learn to compromise and be content. I will choose one of the cars available in the showroom.'

'As you wish, Mr. Sharma.'

When Mr. Iyer came to know about Mr. Sharma's decision, he was happy that he had finally got an efficient salesperson to work with.

It wasn't long before the showroom witnessed an increase in sales due to Saahil's efforts. His monthly income increased significantly due to the commission gained from the sale of cars.

# Chapter 9

The full moon in the sky and its reflection in the river looked like a pair of twin sisters competing to flaunt their beauty. The river, which was a very short walk away from Varsha's house, and the forest adjoining it were covered in a silvery hue of the full moon. It seemed as if a great magician had kept the element of his next trick covered under a huge piece of silvery cloth, garnering anticipation from his eager audience. A cool breeze blowing through the trees created a rustling sound, thus enhancing the enigma.

Two souls sitting on a small rock by the river were engrossed in this enigma. Varsha was in Saahil's embrace, leaning against him. Her feet dangled in the cool water below, creating ripples across the moon's reflection, making it less beautiful than her twin in the sky.

'It feels so good to be with you. We hardly spend any time together these days. Your work keeps you so busy. Can't you spare just half an hour for me every day?' Varsha asked.

'Don't worry. It's just a matter of a few more months. Once we are married, we will have our own house and all the time in the world to spend with each other.'

'I understand that you are doing everything that's needed to give shape to our future. I don't want to distract you from your work. I just want a few moments of togetherness and happiness with you.'

Saahil kissed Varsha. 'I promise that we will meet every day, no matter what. By the way, what will you do if we fail to get married?'

'I don't know. The thought never occurred to me.'

Both sat silently for a few minutes. This silence was interrupted by the hoot of an owl from some tree nearby. All of a sudden, a horrible thought came to Saahil's mind and he sat upright. He made Varsha look into his eyes and said, 'Promise me one thing – you will never commit suicide, no matter what.'

Varsha laughed. 'Don't worry. I will never do that. I want to live with you. Committing suicide won't serve my purpose.' Her laugh vanished the next moment. In a serious tone, she continued, 'Bhaiya knows very well that I am a very strong girl and I won't do anything of that sort. Perhaps that's why he is taking the liberty of harassing me to this extent. I love him so much. I don't know why he is doing all this to me.'

'What did he do now?'

'I am a strong girl. I know I should not cry. I don't want to cry. But I feel like crying,' Varsha said and started sobbing.

Saahil made a great deal of effort to console and calm Varsha down. Wiping Varsha's tears, Saahil asked, 'What's the matter?'

'Bhaiya is going to organize my engagement, a ring ceremony, with that uneducated, unemployed idle donkey, Alok.'

'No, no, no. He can't do that. After all, I am working day and night to fulfil his demands. As a matter of fact, I am on the verge of fulfilling at least one of them – my income is nearing one lakh rupees per month.'

'I told him the same thing.'

'What was his reply?'

'Bhaiya said he would call off my wedding with Alok any time before the decided date if you manage to fulfil all the criteria.'

'I hope he will keep his promise.'

'But I don't want to get engaged to anyone besides you. Please, do something.'

Saahil looked worried. 'I don't know what to do. When and where will the ring ceremony be held?'

'At our hotel. I don't know why bhaiya is in such a hurry. The ceremony is going to be held in five days. It will be a very small gathering – no one except members of the two families will be present. Bhaiya doesn't want any razzmatazz.'

'Good for us too.'

'Yes. One more thing – bhaiya has asked you to have breakfast with us at our place day after tomorrow.'

'Why?'

'I don't know.'

'His hospitality often proves to be burdensome for me. He reveals something shocking every time he invites me to your place.'

'I feel very hopeless sometimes.'

'I feel the same.'

Saahil hugged Varsha.

The competitive duet between the twin lunar sisters was now obscured by the mischievous act of a cloud. A light drizzle drenched the hitherto dry earth, unleashing a pleasing aroma into the air. The earth was not the only thing that was wet, though. Two pairs of eyes were also on the verge of shedding drops of their own.

Two days later, Saahil found himself back in the living room of Mr. Dev and Varsha's house. *'C for Cowardice, C for Courage - Your attitude makes the difference.'* Saahil looked at the poster in the living room. 'Yes. Courage – that's the word,' Saahil told himself. He thought, 'Today, I will gather enough courage to look straight into Mr. Dev's eyes and tell him that he has got no right to play with our lives. I will warn him to not force Varsha into getting engaged to someone else. He can't act like a dictator.'

'Do you want to say something?' Mr. Dev's heavy voice hammered against Saahil's eardrums. Mr. Dev made himself comfortable in a cozy sofa opposite Saahil. Varsha served ice cream to both of them.

'No. Nothing, sir. Nothing at all. I don't have anything to say. Nothing at all.' All the courage that Saahil had gathered evaporated in a second.

'So, did you like the breakfast?' Mr. Dev asked after he had finished his ice cream.

'Yes. I loved it. It was very tasty and healthy too.'

'Healthy? I don't think it was healthy at all. *Parathas* - fried in ghee, curries - packed with spices and oil, sweets and ice cream - full of calories; I don't find any of these healthy.'

'Of course. Such types of food are detrimental to one's health. These things also arouse the animalistic side of a human. Therefore, one should always take *sattvic* food,' Saahil said, licking the remains of his ice cream from the bowl.

'Could you please ask the animal in you to stop licking the ice cream and rest for a while? I want to talk to the human in you,' Mr. Dev said sternly.

'Oh. Sure.' Saahil kept the bowl aside and wiped his ice cream-smeared lips on his sleeve.

Disgusted at the sight, Mr. Dev whispered to Varsha, 'People say love is blind. Actually, they should say love is a moron.' He then addressed Saahil, 'Varsha must already have told you about the ring ceremony, but it's my duty to inform you about it personally. After all, it's part of the game. I am about to cross the second hurdle.' He waited for Saahil to object and start an argument against his decision, but contrary to his expectation, Saahil remained quiet. Even Varsha didn't say anything. Both of them knew that there was no point in arguing with Mr. Dev.

Perhaps Saahil's silence deprived Mr. Dev of the joy he had expected to gain from an argument. He asked, 'Don't you want to say anything else about the matter?'

'No. I don't want to count the hurdles. My target is to win the game. No one wants to know the number of hurdles a player has crossed. Everyone wants to know who the winner is,' said Saahil.

'Hmm. Only time will tell whether it's confidence or overconfidence.'

'Sir, may I disturb you for a moment?' Mr. Kashyap, Mr. Dev's personal secretary, stood in the doorway, flashing his evergreen (or rather, ever-red) betel juice-stained smile.

'Yes. What's the matter?' Mr. Dev asked.

'A man wants to meet you. He says he is a messenger from Mr. Alok's place.'

'Bring him in.'

After a few moments, a man came in and bowed to Mr. Dev.

Mr. Dev offered him to sit and asked Mr. Kashyap to arrange breakfast for him. The man declined the offer with folded hands, however, and said, 'Sir, please forgive me. Our custom doesn't allow us to have food or water at the would-be bride's place.'

'I understand. So tell me, what brings you here?'

'Sir, a big problem has arisen. Mr. Alok met with an accident yesterday, and has broken his leg.'

'Oh. That's so unfortunate. Let me call him right away.' Mr. Dev looked concerned as he reached for his cell phone.

'Sir, you won't be able to reach him on his phone. The network in our area has not been working since yesterday. That's why they sent me here. Apart from the fracture, Mr. Alok is alright, but it won't be possible for him and his family members to come here to attend the ring ceremony.'

'I am afraid we will have to postpone the ceremony in that case,' Mr. Dev said thoughtfully.

'We consulted our family priest regarding the same, but he said that no other suitable dates are available for the ceremony in the near future.'

'Oh. What should we do then? Should Varsha and I come to your place and have the ceremony there?'

'No, no, sir. Please don't even think of it. The bride cannot enter the groom's place before the wedding. That will be against our customs. In fact, people will treat it as blasphemy.' The messenger touched his ears and stuck his tongue out in order to make Mr. Dev realize the severity of the crime.

'But there must be a solution.' Mr. Dev looked worried.

'Yes. That's why I am here.' The messenger handed Mr. Dev a large brass tray containing something covered in a red cloth. 'Sir, this tray contains some of the things given to the bride during the ring ceremony.'

Mr. Dev removed the red cloth and found the engagement ring, some bangles and other jewellery, a small ivory box containing turmeric powder, a gorgeous red bridal dress and a few other articles placed neatly on the tray.

The messenger continued, 'If you give me the engagement ring that you have got for Mr. Alok, I will deliver it to him. On the scheduled date of the ring ceremony, the groom and the bride may wear the rings by themselves, if you don't have any objection to it. Our family priest will carry out the minimum possible rituals at our place. By this means, we will be able to hold the ring ceremony without either the bride or the groom having to travel to each other's place. However, Mr. Alok has insisted that all this will be done only if you permit it.'

Mr. Dev thought for a moment and said, 'That's a nice proposal, I think. I don't see any reason to disagree.' He brought Alok's engagement ring from his room, handed it to the messenger and said, 'Please convey my regards to Mr. Alok.'

'I will, sir. I will have to start my journey now.' The messenger rose from his seat and bowed to everyone with folded hands.

Mr. Dev walked the messenger to the doorway, then returned to Varsha, gave her the large tray given by the messenger and said, 'I want to see the engagement ring on your finger on the scheduled date of the ceremony.'

'But...' Varsha tried to say something.

She was stopped by Mr. Dev. 'I don't want any arguments or excuses.' He then shook hands with Saahil. Saahil understood that it was Mr. Dev's silent and polite way of saying, 'Now, get lost.'

It was yet another moonlit night. The rivalry between the twin moon-sisters was intense. Saahil and Varsha were lying supine on the cool sand of the riverbank, gazing at the endless starlit sky. Saahil wondered whether those stars ever got bored of doing the same thing every day – nothing except winking at each other.

Varsha asked Saahil, 'Do you think what we just did was right?'

'Of course. There was nothing wrong in it.'

'I am feeling a little guilty. I have never taken any major step in my life without bhaiya's knowledge. Today, I am feeling like I cheated bhaiya.'

'You think we should have asked for Mr. Dev's permission and he would have allowed you to get engaged to me? Never. That's why we did it secretly. We have not committed any crime. We have only exchanged our rings and have gotten engaged to each other. It ought to be one of the happiest days of our life. Instead of feeling guilty, we should relish these moments of happiness.' Saahil hugged Varsha affectionately.

Varsha smiled. 'You are right. We haven't done anything wrong. Moreover, now that we are engaged, I am more positive and hopeful about our wedding. It's a wonderful feeling. I was your girlfriend a few minutes ago, and now I am your fiancé. I love this feeling. I love you…a lot.' They kissed.

Saahil said, 'Be careful not to let Mr. Dev see the ring on your finger today. He wants to see the engagement ring on your finger on the scheduled date of the ring ceremony. Tomorrow is the day. Don't show him the ring on your finger before tomorrow. One more thing - you have not cheated your brother. He had said, "the engagement ring" and not "the engagement ring given by Alok." So, you have not cheated him, even though you are wearing the engagement ring given by me.'

Varsha was surprised. 'Given by you? You mean, the ring I am wearing right now is not the one given by Alok?'

'Yes. You are right. After I took the ring from you, I went to a jeweller and asked him to make another ring of the same design and weight at the earliest. He obliged and made me the one that you are wearing now. I couldn't let you wear an engagement ring given by someone else, and I didn't want Mr. Dev to suspect you by seeing a different ring on your finger either.' Saahil produced a small jewellery box from his pocket and opened it. 'Here is the ring given by Alok.'

With her mouth agape, Varsha stared at both the rings shining in the moonlight. 'The ring must have cost you a lot. There was no need to spend so much.'

'Yes, there was. You are mine. You cannot wear an engagement ring given by someone else.'

'I love you.' Varsha showered Saahil with kisses.

# Chapter 10

It was a Sunday. Saahil and Vaibhav ventured into the risky business of cleaning their room – fighting against spiders, termites, mosquitoes and cockroaches. The creatures had found rent-free shelter in the room since a long time ago, but Vaibhav had accepted it as a symbiotic relationship. The creatures got free food and shelter, and in return, they kept Vaibhav company.

Vaibhav always liked to have lazy Sundays. When Saahil first asked him to help him clean the room, Vaibhav said, 'Drop the idea and go back to sleep. Let's not harm and torture these innocent creatures. We shouldn't disturb the ecosystem of this room. Moreover, I have some moral responsibility towards animal conservation.'

It cost Saahil only a can of beer to get Vaibhav engaged in moral turpitude. Vaibhav then said in justification, 'Well, it's not wrong to do pest control.' Soon, he was found running after the frightened cockroaches and the panic-stricken spiders, with an old magazine rolled into a cylinder in his hand.

After an hour long battle, a heap of cockroaches and spiders – some dead, some injured, some unconscious, and some comatose – was found at the doorway. Another heap that contained a lot of useless things was on the floor next to Vaibhav's bed. When Saahil started to stuff them into a trash bag, Vaibhav restrained him and said, 'I need to keep some of these things. I have some sweet memories attached to them.'

'Oh! I didn't know you had emotions too. By the way, whose memories are those?' Saahil asked.

'My ex-girlfriend,' Vaibhav replied.

Saahil was shocked. 'Oh! New revelation. You never told me that you had a girlfriend!'

'You never asked me.' Vaibhav started gathering a few things from the heap – a skipping rope, a stainless steel bowl, a handkerchief, a piece of plastic and an electric switch.

'All these things belonged to her?' Saahil asked.

'No, all these things belong to me. but she had touched them. So her memories are attached to them through her touch.'

Saahil was curious to know the love story of a guy who had the emotional bandwidth of a stone. He kept the polythene bag aside and sat near Vaibhav. 'Come on, tell me everything from the beginning. How did it all happen?'

Vaibhav held the things which he had gathered close to his heart and started with a smile, 'I was visiting home during my summer vacation, and this girl lived in our neighborhood. One day, the girl rang our doorbell by pressing this switch. She had brought some sweets for us in this stainless steel bowl. Her mother had sent some sweets for us. She handed the bowl to my mother and wiped her hands on my handkerchief which was lying on the sofa then. When my mother went to the other room in order to bring some sweets to give to her in return, she sat on a plastic chair kept nearby. This piece of plastic belonged to that chair. Then, she smiled at me and started fiddling with my skipping rope which was also lying on the sofa. I still remember her enchanting smile.' Vaibhav showed Saahil all the things one by one, starting from the switch of the doorbell to the skipping rope, as he went on narrating the story.

'What happened next?' Saahil asked enthusiastically.

'My mother gave her some sweets and she left.'

'Okay. When did you meet her again? How did you people fall in love? What happened after that? Tell me everything,' Saahil said.

'I have already told you everything,' Vaibhav said, keeping the things safely in his cupboard.

'Wait a minute - you mean you never met her again and nothing happened between you two after that?'

'That's right.'

Saahil's enthusiasm vanished at once. 'Are you crazy? Where is the love story in this? How can you even call her your girlfriend?'

'Ex-girlfriend.'

'Whatever. The point is, she was never your girlfriend.'

'I didn't say she was ever my girlfriend. She is my ex-girlfriend. Here "ex" stands for "expected". I expect that she will be my girlfriend one day.'

Saahil lost his patience. 'Actually, you are not crazy. I was crazy enough to waste my time listening to your useless story. Let's get back to work and finish it quickly. After that, I have to leave in search of a new house.'

'Why? Don't you want to stay with me anymore? I promise I will try to keep the room as clean as possible.'

'You don't understand. I have fulfilled one of the conditions set by Mr. Dev. My monthly income is more than one lakh rupees these days. Now, I need to look for a nice house to own – the second condition set by Mr. Dev.'

'Fine. Let's finish the cleaning job quickly. I will accompany you in your search, if you want.'

'That will be helpful, in fact. One of my friends has given me the address of a real estate broker.'

Two hours later, they were standing in a narrow stinky street in the outskirts of the city. The address slip that Saahil had mentioned no house number. After enquiring form a few people, they finally found a child who led them to the real estate broker's place. His residence was not even a house, but a huge Hume pipe partitioned in the middle by a curtain. The broker was at that moment cooking something on a firewood stove kept on one side inside the hume pipe. The child addressed him, 'These men want to meet you.'

The broker looked up at Saahil and Vaibhav, wiped his hands on a dirty towel and came out of the Hume pipe. 'Yes, what can I do for you?' he asked.

Saahil was not sure whether he had found the right person, or if he should even tell him the purpose of his visit, for he didn't seem like he could be of any help. Hesitatingly, he said, 'I am in search of a nice house. A friend told me that you could help.'

'Definitely. You want it on rent, right?'

'No. I want to buy one.'

The broker looked at Saahil and his bicycle with disbelief, then said, 'Fine. Let's go to my office. My house is a bit messy.' He pointed back at the Hume pipe inside which he had been cooking his food. 'Moreover, I don't discuss official matters at home. Please come with me.' He put out the fire under the stove and returned.

Vaibhav whispered to Saahil, 'Thank God, at least he has an office to sit in.'

Walking by the side of the Hume pipe, the broker led them to its other end, the portion that had been segregated off by the curtain. Pointing to that portion, he said, 'Gentlemen, this is my office.' This part of the tiny cylindrical enclosure had a dirty carpet spread on the floor. A few old diaries and two pens were lying in one corner of it.

The broker invited them, 'Please come inside. Don't mind the shortage of space. After all, this is called space management. See how beautifully I have managed to accommodate both my home and office inside a Hume pipe. You see, it's so difficult to get a good house at a reasonable price these days. I have been searching for a house for myself these last seven years, but I haven't got one till today. I have been living here all this while. Take my advice and stop thinking of buying a house. There are many more options available at cheaper prices.'

'Options like?' Vaibhav asked.

'You can choose a place according to your preference. If you love urban life, you can choose a Hume pipe, just like I have. If you are the adventurous type, you can opt for a tent. A hut will fulfil your needs if you are concerned about safety and privacy. If you are a nature lover, you can go for a green-shelter. I can provide you any of these at a very cheap price.'

Saahil looked perplexed at the prospect of living in any of these. Vaibhav asked, 'What is a green-shelter?'

'It's the simplest and cheapest form of shelter. I will help you find a large banyan tree. You can spread a carpet under it and live there. The only expense will be that of buying a carpet. Enjoy the beauty of nature at minimal cost – dual benefit, you see.'

Saahil and Vaibhav looked at each other. 'Please excuse us for a minute,' said Vaibhav to the broker. He dragged Saahil away and whispered, 'Is this person mad? No, no. In fact, I think your friend who gave you the reference of this broker must be mad. The broker actually expects you to live under a tree or in a Hume pipe? Why are we wasting our time listening to the crap he is dishing out to us?'

By now, the broker had incited an inferiority complex in Saahil, so much so that he started suspecting his own ability to buy a house. He asked, 'Vaibhav, look at me carefully and tell me the truth – do I look like a beggar or a vagabond? Do you think I can even really buy a house in my life?'

Vaibhav replied, 'See, you have already started to contract the broker's madness. Let's leave this place before it engulfs you completely.'

As they started to leave, the broker asked, 'What happened?'

Vaibhav replied, 'Hearing of so many options, my friend has got a bit confused. He needs time to decide which one he should go for. We will inform you as soon as he decides.'

As they hurried to leave, they heard the broker say, 'You have got one more option. I am looking for a roommate to share this Hume pipe with. Let me know if you are interested.'

They rode their bicycles as fast as they could in order to get away from the broker as soon as possible.

When they returned to their room, Vaibhav said, 'We should have enquired about the broker before meeting him. We should do our homework before we meet a broker next time. Give me two days. I will do a thorough research about the real-estate in our city. We will then embark again on our house-finding mission.'

'Alright.' Saahil had not yet emerged out of the inferiority complex induced depression.

After two days, Vaibhav carefully picked a real-estate broker after thorough research. When they set out to meet the broker, Vaibhav said, 'This time, I am all prepared to defeat the broker.'

Saahil grew a bit concerned. 'Hello, we are not going on a war. We are merely going to search for a house. I hope you will remember that.'

'Yes, of course,' Vaibhav assured Saahil.

The office of this real-estate broker turned out to be a decent one, though it was not huge. The broker welcomed Saahil and Vaibhav. 'How can I help you?' he asked.

Vaibhav said, 'My friend wants to buy a house.' In order to leave no scope for any absurd options like a Hume pipe or a green-shelter, he added, 'Let me make myself clear – by 'a house', I mean a place built of bricks and cement, with rooms, walls, a roof, doors and windows.'

The broker looked a bit confused. 'Of course, I know what a house is, sir.'

Vaibhav whispered to Saahil, 'See, he knows what a house is. This proves that on the basis of my research, I have brought you to the right person.'

Saahil whispered back, 'Oh! What a genius he is! After all, he knows what a house is.'

The broker asked, 'Are you looking for a 2 BHK house or a 3 BHK house?'

Vaibhav replied, 'My friend doesn't have a huge budget, so a 2 BHK house will do. But the point is that it should meet our requirements.'

'Anything specific?'

'Yes. The house should be located in a posh area of the city, but it should not be expensive.'

'How is that possible, sir? A house in a posh area is likely to be expensive.'

'That's why we have come to you. It's your job to find a house that meets our requirements.'

'I will try, sir, but I can't guarantee. Is there anything more you want to add?'

'Round the clock water and electricity supply.'

'That goes without saying, sir.'

'The society should have security guards, a swimming pool, a gym, a park, a parking lot, a club house and Wi-Fi facility,' Vaibhav added.

'But the house shouldn't be expensive in spite of all these amenities, right?' the broker said somewhat irritatedly.

Vaibhav said, 'Right. The house should be fully furnished with an air-conditioner, TV, kitchen appliances, furniture...'

The broker interrupted, 'But the house shouldn't be expensive, right?' He tried not to lose his temper.

'Right. And the most important thing – it's about the shape of the house.'

'Shape?'

'Yes. The house should be either pyramidal or spherical in shape,' Vaibhav replied.

'What?' The broker rose up from his chair.

Vaibhav explained, 'Yes. Pyramids and spheres are the most stable and strong structures logically, and we want the house to be strong.'

The broker kept silent for a minute in order to control his anger, then said, 'The only accommodation of a pyramidal shape that I can provide you is a tent. Are you interested?'

'Are you joking?' Vaibhav grew angry.

'Why can't I joke when you are?' The broker was equally angry.

Saahil, who had been silent till now, saw the situation getting out of control and sent Vaibhav out. He then apologized to the broker. 'Actually, my friend has lost it. Please don't mind his words. I will come to meet you alone some other time.' As he left, quite depressed, he muttered, 'Every broker offers me a tent to live in. I think that's the only accommodation my fate has in store for me.'

Frustrated with the two disastrous house-hunt adventures, Saahil asked Varsha one day, 'How much do you love me?'

'More than my own life.' Varsha responded, almost mechanically.

'What would you do for me?' Saahil asked.

'Anything. I would die for you.' Another practiced answer came promptly.

Overwhelmed by Varsha's response, Saahil asked enthusiastically, 'Would you live with me in a tent?'

Another answer came promptly, 'No way. I can die for you, but when it comes to living, I can't live in a tent with you. Why are you asking me such an absurd question?'

Saahil told her everything that had happened with the two brokers and said, 'Now, I have a strong feeling that a tent is the only accommodation my fate has in store for me.'

Varsha said, 'You are worrying unnecessarily. I know someone who can help us. People call him *Makaan bhai*.'

'Makaan bhai? What kind of a name is that?'

'No one knows his real name. Everyone calls him by that name because he provides suitable *makaan* (houses) to people.'

Varsha called up Makaan bhai, told him everything and fixed an appointment for the next day.

When Saahil and Varsha went to meet Makaan bhai at his office the next day, he welcomed them and said, 'We should prepare a tent—'

'No,' Saahil almost shouted. 'A tent is out of question. How can we live in a tent? We can't manage in a tent. Please don't suggest a tent to us.'

Makaan bhai looked surprised. 'Of course not, sir. I know Varsha madam's social status. How can I dare to suggest a tent to her? Moreover, I am a real estate broker. I provide houses, not tents. I just wanted to say that we should prepare a tentative list of specifications for your dream house before we proceed to search for it.'

'Oh!' Saahil felt relieved. He detailed to him what their dream house should be like.

Makaan bhai said, 'Now, let me show you some houses. We can drive to the sites in my car.'

The first site they drove to was a huge rice paddy spread across acres of land. Varsha said to Saahil, 'I don't see any houses here.'

Saahil said, 'I think it's a farmhouse. What we are seeing now must be the farm. The house must be somewhere nearby.'

Makaan bhai overheard Saahil and said, 'I am sorry to disappoint you, sir. It's not a farmhouse. In fact, there is no house here. What you are seeing now is the construction site. The construction of houses will start here very soon.'

Saahil asked, 'When?'

'As soon as the bank approves the loan.'

'When will that happen?'

'As soon as the builder applies for the loan.'

'When will he do that?'

'As soon as he gets the conversion and the mutation of the land done. You see, the site is an agricultural land originally.'

'And when is that supposed to happen?'

'As soon as the builder buys the land from the farmer who owns it. The price negotiation is going on, but you don't need to worry. Everything will be finished very soon,' Makaan bhai assured him.

Saahil became impatient. 'We can't wait for years for all these things to happen. We have hardly got a few months to own a house.'

'Oh! I understand. Actually, I brought you here because it costs less when you book a house before it's constructed. Move-in ready houses are quite costly. Anyway, let me show you some move-in ready houses as you don't have much time in hand.'

Makaan bhai then showed them a few move-in ready houses, but the prices were very high as he had warned. Saahil said, 'Makaan bhai, my pocket doesn't allow me to buy such a high-priced house. Can't you suggest me some low-priced move-in ready house?'

Makaan bhai started feeling that he was wasting his time. He said, 'You don't have much time in hand. You don't have much money in hand either. How are you going to buy a house?'

Varsha said, 'Please, Makaan bhai, we need you to help us. It's a matter of our life. Please do something.'

Makaan bhai looked at Varsha and Saahil. He could see helplessness in their eyes. Something in those desperate eyes coerced him to do something to help them. He said, 'When I was a child, we lived in the slums of the city. My parents tried their best to own a small house in some nice part of the city and get us out of the slums, but they failed as they could never save up enough money to own a real house. When my father was about to die, he expressed this regret to us and said, "For some people, a house means luxury; for some, it means investment. But for us, it was a necessity which I could never fulfil." I have been in this business for the last twenty years. I can differentiate between luxury and necessity. I will try to help you people. I can't guarantee anything though.' He didn't hesitate to call his office and asked to postpone all his appointments for the rest of the day.

On the way to their next destination, Makaan bhai said, 'I am going to show you some more move-in ready houses that are cheaper than those you have already seen till now. I would like to mention one thing here though. These houses are cheaper because all of them have got some negative features. Nevertheless, positive and negative are relative terms. Something that seems negative to someone might not be all that bad from your point of view. It will be better if you see the houses yourself and then decide.'

They drove along a relatively deserted road. Finally, Makaan bhai stopped his car in front of a house that could be called a mini bungalow. The house looked so untidy and dirty from outside that one could easily guess that it was deserted. Some of its windows were broken or cracked. The walls had several tortuous cracks running along them, providing unauthorized refuge to the roots of a few small plants. An eerie atmosphere weighed heavy over the house.

Before they stepped out of the car, Varsha said, 'It looks like the houses they show in horror movies.'

Makaan bhai confirmed, 'You guessed it right, madam. They say this house is haunted. That's why no one buys it. That's why this house is so cheap.'

'What? I am not going to live in a haunted house. No way!' Varsha's eyes became exceptionally wide with fear as if she had already seen a ghost.

On the other hand, Saahil didn't seem too bothered by it. He was curious instead. He asked, 'By the way, is the house haunted by ghosts or some other creatures of sort?'

Makaan bhai was no less enthusiastic to quench Saahil's curiosity. 'Some people say it's the ghost of one of the old occupants of the house that haunts this place. Others believe that a mischievous jinn has made the house its abode since a long time ago.'

Saahil probed further. 'What's the difference between a ghost and a jinn?'

Makaan bhai didn't want to let go of the opportunity to show off his knowledge of the supernatural. He started, 'You see, a ghost is the soul of a dead person, whereas a jinn is a living supernatural entity that is capable of possessing humans. There exist some other supernatural entities like zombies, witches...'

Makaan bhai's words were aggravating Varsha's fear, but she was not in a position to be rude to him, so she targeted Saahil. 'Saahil, can you please postpone your inquiry regarding the classification of ghosts for some time? And can we please move away from this creepy place right now?'

Makaan bhai realized that he was deviating from the real motive of their journey. He apologized, 'It's my fault. Let's proceed to see the other houses.' Makaan bhai took pains to show them as many as eight more houses, but each of the houses had something against it that prevented Varsha and Saahil from deciding in favor of it.

All three of them were equally frustrated by the end of the expedition. The sun was also about to end its expedition for the day. Having skipped their lunch, they felt ravenous with hunger. Failing to ignore the repeated appeals made by his stomach, Makaan bhai finally suggested that they take something to pacify their revolting stomachs. As no restaurant could be expected to provide them lunch at that time of the day, they had to soothe their hunger pangs with tea and buns at a small roadside tea stall.

Evening was soon approaching. For some reason, Saahil always found the setting sun very depressing. The failure of their expedition that day added to it.

Makaan bhai sensed the depression in the young couple's eyes and tried to lighten the situation by joking. 'You see, our effort today was not all in vain. At least, we lost some calories by skipping lunch and running around the city.' As he had expected, the joke fell flat and was unable to wipe away the gloom from his listeners' faces.

Makaan bhai dipped his bun in the tea, took a bite and continued, 'When I was a child, I hated eating buns because our poverty didn't allow us to have a standard dinner every night. This is all we had most nights – one bun and a glass of water for each. My younger brother, who was just a boy of five at the time, was unable to understand the economy of one bun and a glass of water. He would ask for more buns. My mother would feed him her share of the bun and go to bed on an empty stomach. I hated to see her do it, but there was nothing I could do to earn more money. I hated my helplessness. Actually, I hated the tragedy of our life that revolved around the buns, and not the buns themselves. I promised myself that I would earn a lot of money when I grew up so that my family and I would never have to eat buns again. I worked day and night to reach where I am today. I remain so busy that often I don't get the time to have a standard lunch or dinner, like it happened today. Ultimately, I soothe my hunger by taking these buns – the same that I hated so much in my childhood. I don't hate eating them so much these days. Maybe it's because eating buns is not an obligation for me and my family anymore; it's just an option. My experience with buns has taught me three lessons – First, it's no use trying to change everything that we don't like. Some things are just a part of life, so it's better to learn to live with them instead of going on complaining. Second, things and situations aren't always as bad as we think. Third, with effort and perseverance, we can turn bad situations into good ones one day.' Makaan bhai took another bite of his bun with utmost content.

Saahil looked at the bun he was holding and asked with hope, 'You mean to say that we may succeed in our house hunt expedition one day?'

'Undoubtedly,' Makaan bhai replied.

Saahil and Varsha kept their cups aside and started listening more attentively.

Makaan bhai said, 'Remember the third lesson - through effort and perseverance, we can turn bad situations into good ones one day. Let's start thinking about your problem afresh. You have got two main issues – lack of time and lack of money. You haven't got enough time in hand to wait for an under-construction house to get built fully. So, the only option left is a ready to move-in house. I will have to make some more effort to search for a few more cheap, move-in ready houses. Give me a week's time. I will show you some more houses. Even if you don't like any of them completely, you may buy one for the time being. You can sell it later when you have more money in hand to buy a better house.'

Varsha said, 'Hmm. Not a bad idea.'

Makaan bhai said, 'Now, let's talk about the funds. Do you have enough money in hand to pay the price of the house in a lump-sum?'

'No,' Saahil replied.

'You will need a bank loan in that case. Still, you must have some money in hand to make the down payment.'

Saahil's reply was a 'no' again. 'I don't have much money. You see, my business has started to prosper only recently.'

Even Makaan bhai felt a bit discouraged at this stage hearing so many 'no's. 'You must be joking. You are searching for a house to buy with almost no money in hand!' The very next moment, another doubt forced Makaan bhai to raise his eyebrows. 'Do you at least have the documents that are required to get a loan?'

'Documents like?'

'Like your proof of identity, proof of address, last three years' balance sheet of your business, last three years' income tax returns, etc.' Makaan bhai looked at Saahil expectantly for an answer.

A long period of silence prevailed following the question. Saahil finally replied with a sense of criminal guilt. 'I have started my business only a few months back, so I haven't got all the documents.'

Makaan bhai stared at Saahil and Varsha. Another spell of silence prevailed. It was difficult to say who of the three felt the most dejected in that moment. Finally, Varsha asked, 'What do we do now?'

Makaan bhai, who had lost all hope by now, let out a sigh of frustration and said, 'Follow the first lesson that I learned from my experience with the buns - It's no use trying to change everything that we don't like. Some things are just a part of life. It's better to learn to live with them instead of going on complaining.'

# Chapter 11

Only two days had passed after their disastrous house-hunt adventure when Varsha met Saahil with a huge grin on her face. Saahil couldn't quite understand the reason behind her happiness. It always bewildered him when people said that two persons in love could understand each other's feelings even without uttering a single word. Varsha was like a foreign language movie for Saahil – impossible to understand even with the audio on, sometimes incomprehensible in spite of the subtitles. How could he ever hope to understand her feelings with no audio even?

'Why are you so happy?' he enquired. 'Buying a house seems like an impossible dream for us right now. I don't see any reason for us to be happy.'

Varsha's enthusiasm remained unabated. She revealed to him Mr. Dev's debit card and said, 'Bhaiya has asked me to do the shopping for our wedding.'

'You mean your wedding, right?' Saahil was irked.

Varsha tried to console him. 'No. I mean our wedding. I am not going to marry anyone except you. Whatever bhaiya may have in his mind, I know what wedding I am shopping for. Come on, smile now. After all, we are going to shop for *our wedding*,' she winked.

Saahil tried to fake a smile, but failed. He still couldn't find it in him a reason to be truly happy. For Varsha, however, shopping had always been a great reason to smile. She was ten times more enthusiastic and particular than any average girl when it came to shopping. Saahil didn't want to spoil her optimism about their wedding, so he asked, 'What all are we going to shop for?'

'Everything – clothes, shoes, cosmetics, apparels, jewellery – everything.' Varsha was overwhelmed with enthusiasm.

Saahil just smiled, but his self-respect was getting hurt by the prospect of buying things for himself with Mr. Dev's money. Varsha took out one more debit card from her purse. 'This is my debit card. We can use it for buying things for you. I know you won't like to spend bhaiya's money on yourself. Now, don't tell me that you can't use my debit card either. After all, it's not my money; it's our money.'

Saahil looked at Varsha in astonishment. wondering how she could have known what he felt, even though he hadn't uttered a word. Perhaps it was true, he thought, that people in love knew each other's feelings even without being told a word. Perhaps it was he who had been stupid enough to think that Varsha was like a foreign language movie. He smiled again and said, 'But your debit card won't be of any use while buying things for me.'

'Why?'

'I buy locally-made shoes from Natthu cobbler. I get my trousers and shirts stitched by Jumman bhai tailor. I buy my watches for only a few bucks from Baalu who deals in second-hand and locally-made goods. And none of these people accept debit cards.'

'But you are certainly not going to wear things bought from them at our wedding. Let's get going instead of wasting time here.'

Saahil guessed that shopping with Varsha was going to be a tough job. He had seen couples going shopping before, but it was nothing compared to what Varsha did that day.

When the salesperson showed her something expensive, Varsha said, 'It's too expensive. Show me something else.'

Then the salesperson produced something that had a discount on it, to which Varsha frowned and said, 'An item with a discount is never reliable. You people provide discounts and offers only when you need to dispose of old and inferior-quality products. You can't fool me with discounts and offers. Show me good-quality products.'

Then, trying to find a balance between quality and economy, the salesperson thoroughly searched the racks behind him and produced an item of the average standard. Varsha probed, 'What about the warranty?'

'One year's warranty, madam.'

'What? Only one year? That means the company knows that the product will not last for more than a year. A company provides warranty for a short term only when it's not sure of the longevity of the product. Show me something else – one with a longer warranty period.'

The salesperson again showed something expensive, of course, with a longer warranty period.

'I have already told you not to show me very expensive items!' Varsha said.

The salesperson felt helpless and looked at Saahil with a hope that he would sympathize with him and interfere in the matter. Little did he know that Saahil was as helpless as he was at the moment.

The only thing that Varsha purchased after a whole day of torturous shopping was a blue velvet evening gown. She had visited four different malls and tried at least twenty different gowns before she made up her mind to purchase that particular blue gown. She updated her status with a photo on social media every time she tried on a new gown. At least a hundred people had opined over the gowns she tried, and she gave due importance to the public opinion while selecting the gown.

When Varsha finally purchased the gown, Saahil thought that the day wasn't a complete waste after all, but he didn't know that the task wasn't over yet. When they were talking over a cup of coffee in a restaurant that evening, Varsha asked, 'Are you sure that the gown I bought looks good?'

'Undoubtedly. It looks nice. In fact, it's gorgeous,' Saahil assured.

'Yes, I agree. But the material...you know...it feels like it sticks to my body too much,' Varsha said with a hint of displeasure in her voice.

'But you look very nice in it. In fact, I should say that the gown looks very nice on you.' Saahil tried to console her.

Varsha didn't seem impressed. 'You may be right, but do you remember the red gown – the one with very small white flowers on it? I think that one looked better.'

'Why didn't you get that one then?'

'How about the purple one with wavy pattern?' Varsha began to get enthusiastic again.

'Which one? I don't remember...'

'The pink chiffon gown also looked gorgeous. I think I should have gotten that one instead of this dull blue gown.' Varsha spilt some coffee as she got excited.

'But...' Saahil didn't know what to say.

'No, wait. The green one with golden embroidery looked unique. I think I will buy that one.'

'But...' Saahil got scared as Varsha used the simple future tense of the verb "buy". He knew he couldn't stand another day of torturous shopping. He tried to restrain Varsha from going to shop for another gown, saying, 'No, no. You look absolutely stunning in that blue gown. You don't need another one.'

'Certainly, I am not going to get one more gown,' Varsha said. Saahil felt relieved for a moment, only to panic again when Varsha added, 'I will just exchange this blue gown for a better one.'

Saahil didn't know how futile it was to try to restrain a girl from going shopping, and he kept on trying. 'Exchange? But the salesperson mentioned it clearly that no exchange was allowed.'

'Oh, never mind such cautionary notices, they are only for male customers like you. Shopping is an art mastered by girls. When the customer is a girl like me, an invisible treaty always exists between the shop and the customer. The treaty says that the customer can exchange anything anytime. Leave it to me. I know how to handle this. '

'Do you mean to say that you can do it yourself?'

'Yes.'

'You mean, you don't need me to accompany you this time?' Saahil kept his fingers crossed under the table, hoping for Varsha to answer in his favor.

'Of course, that's what I mean. I have already wasted your day enough. I don't want to waste your time any more. I know you are trying to devote most of your time to your work in order to make our future better. I can do the rest of the shopping myself. I will send you the photos or call you in case of any doubt. I had asked you to accompany me today so I could spend some time with you,' Varsha smiled.

Saahil refrained from pointing out that it was not him but the salespersons with whom Varsha had spent most of her time that day. He was just happy that he was now free from performing the horrible task. He felt like celebrating and ordered a full-sized pizza.

His gaze returned to Varsha and he felt like he was seeing her after many days. He realized that he had not spent a single second in the past few days to actually look at her. He couldn't remember when he had held her hands last, when he had hugged her last, or when he had kissed her last. She had been with him all day, but he had not been with her, not even for a second. His mind had perpetually been occupied with the problems of his profession.

He rose from his chair instantly, called the waiter and cancelled the order. He grabbed Varsha's hand and said, 'Let's go shopping. Again. Now."

Varsha was surprised. 'Now?'

'Yes. Now. We will first go and get the blue gown exchanged.'

Varsha giggled. 'I thought you had gotten bored of shopping!'

'I got bored of shopping, not of you.'

When they entered the mall again, they found the salesperson who had sold the blue gown to Varsha busy talking to a man who, from his attire, seemed to be the manager of the showroom. Varsha approached them with a huge smile on her face. 'Excuse me, gentlemen.'

The salesperson was definitely not happy to see a terrible shopper like Varsha return. Nevertheless, he tried to fake a smile. 'Yes, madam, what can I do for you?'

'Nothing. I just came back to thank you people for having named your store to my advantage.'

The manager and the salesperson exchanged confused glances.

Varsha explained, 'I came across my numerologist on my way home. She told me that the name of your store is very lucky for me. She advised me to do all the shopping for my wedding here. Actually, I was silly enough not to ask for her advice beforehand. After all, shopping worth lakhs of rupees is not a small matter. How could I be so careless? Anyway, I am happy that I have come to the right place now, unknowingly though.'

The mention of shopping worth lakhs of rupees made the manager's pupils dilate. It was not easy to get such high-profile customers after all. With a huge smile on his face, he tried to flatter Varsha. 'The pleasure is ours, madam. We are honored to have an esteemed customer like you.' He asked a boy to get coffee for Saahil and her. Then, he continued, 'The mall is all yours, madam. What else would you like to see?'

'Oh, no, no. I'm very tired today. Moreover, it won't be possible for me to shop for all the things I need in only a couple of hours. I will need at least two to three days. I will come tomorrow.'

'As you wish, madam,' the manager said, taking good care not to curtail the dimensions of his smile.

'And yes, one more thing. My numerologist told me that I shouldn't buy anything blue in color until my wedding is over.' Varsha then showed him the blue gown. 'I didn't know that when I bought this gown today. I can't keep the gown with me anymore. I understand that your store doesn't allow an exchange of sold items, so I am not asking for an exchange or a refund. I just want you to take this gown back.'

'As you wish, madam.' The salesperson repeated the manager's words and took the gown from Varsha.

However, the manager knew that a gown had no value in comparison with lakhs of rupees. He looked at the salesperson angrily. 'You people never learn how to behave with esteemed customers.' He then addressed Varsha, 'Exchange and refund policies are for ordinary customers, madam, not for an esteemed customer like you. Please feel free to take any other gown of any other color in exchange for the blue gown.'

'Are you sure?'

'Of course, madam. We will be happy to serve you,' the manager said.

'Oh, that's so nice of you,' Varsha smiled.

The manager ordered the salesperson to show Varsha some more gown options. Varsha chose another gown after a few more cycles of inspection, trial and rejection. She then thanked the manager and the salesperson again.

While leaving the mall, Saahil said to Varsha, 'I agree now that shopping is an art mastered by girls. Will you really do all the shopping for our wedding at this place?'

'Not necessarily. Sometimes, my numerologist does change her opinion,' said Varsha and smiled mischievously.

# Chapter 12

One fine evening – no, wait – using the word 'fine' so loosely might do injustice to Varsha, since the evening was definitely not *fine* for her. So then – one evening, Varsha reached home and found Mr. Dev sitting in the drawing room, a number of sample wedding-invitation cards spread on the table before him.

Mr. Dev said, 'You have come at the right time. I have got these samples from various invitation-card suppliers. Come, help me choose the best one. You see, one can guess how lavish the wedding would be just by looking at the quality of the invitation card. It is the primary most important part of the wedding.'

'Is it more important than even the people who are supposed to get married?' Varsha asked. She couldn't stand the prospect of her name getting printed with any name other than 'Saahil'.

Mr. Dev avoided eye contact with Varsha as he perfectly understood what she meant. He remained adhering to the topic. 'See, how beautiful these cards are! I don't know which one to select. I am quite confused. I need your opinion.'

'Does my opinion really matter to you?' Varsha launched another verbal missile at him, and took the stairs to her room.

As she entered her room, she found her dinner kept on the table beside her bed. She used to have dinner with Mr. Dev in the dining room earlier, but for the last few months, she had been avoiding it. She had decided to make him realize how it felt when one was forced to stay away from one's most loved one. She herself hated staying away from her brother though. She had asked the cook to keep her dinner in her room every evening.

Varsha didn't feel like having dinner that evening. She went straight to the bathroom, took a quick shower and changed into her nightdress. She switched all the lights off, lounged in the recliner next to the window and looked out.

During daytime, the window allowed a picturesque view of the nearby forest and river. In the evenings, Varsha always preferred to keep the window shut and draped, as the same view became scary to her in darkness. Silhouettes of huge trees against the moonlit sky looked like monsters and ghosts.

But today, Varsha had opened the window so as to allow her room to soak in all the darkness of the forest. Today, the darkness seemed very soothing, even caring, perhaps because it didn't leave any scope for discrimination between things – the rich and the poor, the orphaned and the parented.

A gust of mischievous, cool breeze rushed in through the window and kissed Varsha's tender soul. It was followed shortly by freezing cold drops of rain. Varsha didn't shut the window. She let the rain caress her from head to toe. Soon, it started raining heavily, but that made no difference to Varsha. She was in no mood to resist anything today. She had grown tired of resisting. She let in everything that tried to come in – the darkness, the breeze, the rain. She let go of everything that tried to emerge – her fear and her tears.

The rain and the darkness engulfed her body in its entirety. Unaware of the fact, her soul let itself get engulfed by the thoughts of Saahil.

The prospect of her marriage with Saahil was as dark as the forest. There was less than three months' time in hand, but there were three more targets to be achieved – a house, a car and a huge bank balance. Difficult? No. It was not difficult. It was just impossible, she felt. It was no use living in delusion. It was better to accept the truth. She never gave in to getting depressed because she had read somewhere that depression was the slowest method of suicide. But today, she succumbed to it.

Her cell phone rang and she rose out of the trance to find herself drenched from head to toe. The flickering screen of her cell phone displayed Saahil's name. She didn't want anyone to interrupt her thoughts about Saahil at the moment, not even Saahil himself. She let the phone continue to ring until the line was cut off.

However, she didn't know what she had missed by not receiving the call.

She realized that she was shivering with cold. She rose from the recliner and closed the window. She wiped herself dry and changed into another nightdress. When she went to bed and got under the quilt, the warmth reminded her of Saahil's embrace.

Her eyes got wet again. She longed for her mother, perhaps for the first time in her life. Had her mother been alive, she would have wiped her tears at least. The very thought gave rise to more tears. Varsha sobbed and sobbed, and didn't realise when her sobs converted into snores.

When she woke up in the morning, she felt a bit feverish.

The first thing that she remembered from the previous night was Saahil's call, which she had left unattended. She frantically searched for her phone and found it on the teapoy next to the recliner. The phone had been rain-bathed completely and was dead. She made a few unsuccessful attempts to bring it back to life. Frustrated of the result, she threw on a pair of jeans and a T-shirt, and rushed downstairs to call Saahil from the landline.

She paused for a moment to think why she was so worried about Saahil's call. It might have been a casual call after all. But no, she had an intuition that it was not a casual call. To add to her worry, the maid told her that the landline was dead too. She asked the maid, 'May I make an urgent call from your cell phone?'

The maid handed Varsha her phone hesitatingly. 'Madam, my phone has very low balance. We are so poor, you know.'

Varsha knew what she wanted. She handed the maid a hundred bucks. 'Here, keep it. You can get your account recharged later.'

She called Saahil immediately, but Saahil's phone was switched off. She gave the phone back to the maid. She didn't take much time to decide her next move. It was eight o'clock and she knew where to find Saahil at that time. She told the maid, 'Get me my car keys.'

'Madam, as Dev *sahib*'s car didn't start after repeated attempts this morning, he left in your car.'

Varsha felt as if fate was playing pranks with her. In no time, she was on the road, waving for cabs and auto-rickshaws to hire. However, even they seemed to have conspired against her. A number of them passed her by without stopping. Finally, she was able to hire an auto-rickshaw, though it seemed no less appropriate to be kept in an antiques museum. Varsha directed the driver to take her to Saahil's hostel.

She wanted to catch him before he left for his office. Her heart was beating fast, she didn't know why. The auto-rickshaw's pace was inversely proportional to Varsha's heart rate though. She asked the driver, 'Can you drive a little faster?'

'Yes, madam, I can,' replied the driver, but Varsha couldn't feel the speed increasing at all. She repeated herself, 'Can you drive faster?'

'Was that a question or an instruction, madam?' asked the confused driver.

'A request.' Varsha concealed her anger and tried to be as gentle as possible.

'Madam, I said I could drive faster, but the auto-rickshaw won't move any faster owing to its old age. Lajwanti celebrated her tenth birthday just last month.'

'Who is Lajwanti?'

'My auto-rickshaw.' The driver caressed the rear-view mirror passionately.

'Madam, is this the place you mentioned?' asked the driver. They had come to a halt in front of Saahil's hostel.

'Yes, yes, this is the place.' Varsha jumped out of the auto-rickshaw and asked, 'How much?'

'Eighty rupees, madam,' replied the driver.

Only then did Varsha realize that she had left her purse at home. She decided to ask Saahil for the fare. Asking the driver to wait, she rushed to Saahil's room and opened the door without bothering to knock.

Vaibhav welcomed her with a smile on his face.

Varsha asked, 'Where is Saahil?'

'I have no idea. He hasn't returned since last night,' replied Vaibhav.

Varsha felt her racing heart stop beating at once. 'He has been missing since yesterday! Didn't you try to look for him?' she asked anxiously.

'No. You know, four boys in our area went missing last year, and only one of them was found again after searching. So I thought it was no use searching for Saahil when there was only a twenty-five percent chance of getting success,' Vaibhav replied casually.

Varsha growled, 'You are horrible.' She didn't have time to wait for Vaibhav's reply. She hurried back to the auto-rickshaw and said to the driver, 'I may need to go to some more places. I don't have my purse with me right now, but I promise I will pay you the fare in the end. Is that okay with you?'

The driver, an experienced man in his fifties, didn't see any harm in it. He agreed to Varsha's proposal. She asked him to take her to Saahil's office. Her apprehension had turned into full fledged fear by now. She felt guilty about not having received Saahil's call the night before.

They reached Saahil's office where another disappointment was awaiting her. The office was closed. Varsha found her courage giving in. She was about to cry when she suddenly remembered that she had missed one important place. She instructed the driver to take her to the college library where Mr. Das, one of Saahil's greatest well-wishers, worked as the librarian.

She was panting by the time she reached Mr. Das. 'What happened? What are you so worried about?' he asked as he offered her a glass of water.

'Have you seen Saahil today?' she asked, still panting.

'No. Why are you asking?'

Varsha felt her words getting choked in her throat. Trying hard to hold back her tears, she told everything to Mr. Das.

'Calm down. There is nothing to worry. I will go with you to search for him,' said Mr. Das as he tried to hide how worried he himself was. He thought for a while and said, 'I met him yesterday. He said that he would remain busy today as he had some very important work to do. Perhaps he mentioned something about Mr. Iyer's car showroom. I can't recall exactly. Have you got Mr. Iyer's phone number?'

'No,' Varsha said gloomily.

'Even I don't have his number. Should we go down to his showroom? We may at least get some information about Saahil there,' said Mr. Das.

Varsha just nodded.

Mr. Das asked a subordinate to take care of the library and left in the auto-rickshaw with Varsha. As they proceeded to Mr. Iyer's showroom, Varsha kept an eye on the road, scanning every man and every bicycle with the hope of catching a glimpse of Saahil. Her mind kept telling her, 'Don't listen to your heart. It's making a fool out of you. You won't achieve anything by running from pillar to post without any definite information.' Yet, her heart kept telling her, 'Don't listen to your mind. It's just a materialistic complex of neurons. It will never understand your emotions. Keep trying until you succeed.' As a matter of fact, Varsha knew that her mind was perhaps correct this time.

When they reached Mr. Iyer's car showroom, the first thing that caught their attention was a man shouting at the employees of the showroom. 'That must be Mr. Iyer,' Mr. Das whispered to Varsha.

'How do you know?' Varsha whispered back.

'Saahil had told me that Mr. Iyer keeps yelling at his employees at the showroom,' replied Mr. Das.

'But he seems to be in a very bad mood. Do you think he will help us?'

'Never mind, that's his normal mood,' Mr. Das assured Varsha.

Meeting Mr. Iyer, Mr. Das said, 'Hello, I am Mr. Das and this is Varsha. She is...'

Mr. Das didn't have to finish, for Mr. Iyer said with a smile, 'Saahil often talks about you people. He says that—'

Varsha cut short the formalities and got straight to the point. 'Saahil has been missing since yesterday,' she said and started crying.

Mr. Iyer stood confused for a moment, then laughed heartily the very next. 'Oh! That means either Saahil has a twin brother, or human cloning has been legalized.' He laughed again.

'What...do you...mean?' Varsha managed to ask between her sobs.

Mr. Iyer didn't have to explain. Saahil emerged from a brand new hatchback behind them. With a huge grin on his face, he approached Varsha. As she saw him, she ran towards him with a yelp loud enough to catch the attention of everyone present there.

Confused and anxious, Saahil asked, 'What happened? Why are you crying?'

Varsha cried even louder. 'Can't you see? I was so worried. I thought I lost you. Your cell phone was switched off. You weren't to be found anywhere. No one had seen you since yesterday. Without you, I felt as if I were dead.' Her continuous sobbing had made her voice loud and squeaky. At one point, even Mr. Iyer who had been proud of his thunderous voice didn't hesitate to admit that he had some tough competition in her.

Saahil, who had learned a few golden rules of love by now, didn't make the mistake of pointing out that it was she who hadn't received his call the night before. He apologized instead, 'It was my fault. I forgot to charge my cell phone. I stayed at a friend's place last night. I should have returned to my hostel, or I should have at least informed you.'

Varsha kept on crying regardless.

'You have found me now. Why are you still crying?'

'Can't you see? I am so angry with you. You are very irresponsible and insensible and careless ...' With each of the adjectives she blurted out, she added some more decibels to the magnitude of her voice which was already echoing in the showroom.

Saahil found the opportunity to apologize once again when Varsha paused to recall some more adjectives. He said, 'I am really very sorry. I promise that I will be careful in future. Now, smile. I have good news for you. Come, I have got something to show you.'

Hearing the words "good news", Varsha immediately stopped crying. Saahil took her to the car from which he had emerged just a few minutes ago. 'Do you like this car?' asked Saahil.

'It's nice. It looks trendy,' Varsha admired. 'But right now, I am not interested in the cars your clients intend to buy.'

'I thought you might be interested in a car that I intend to buy.'

'Definitely, but…I mean…are you going to…' Varsha wasn't yet ready to believe that her guess might be correct.

Saahil nodded with a smile on his face. 'Yes, your guess is right. This is the car I intend to buy for us, and I am going to buy it today. I had sent you the photo of the car on your cell phone last night. Perhaps, you missed to have a look at the photo. I had called you in order to ask whether you liked the car or not, but you didn't receive my call. So I thought it wouldn't be a bad idea to buy the car and give you a nice surprise.'

Varsha stood stupefied for a few seconds. Next, she looked at Saahil and the car alternately a few times. Gathering all the energy she had then, she started crying at the top of her voice. All heads in the showroom turned towards her once again.

Saahil was confused. He asked, 'What happened? Did I do something wrong this time? Why are you crying now?'

Varsha stopped crying and said, 'Can't you see? I am so happy right now. I was so tense last night. Now that you have achieved one more target, I can't tell you how happy I am. Now, I feel positive about the possibility of our marriage. I love you. I love you. I love you…' With a huge smile on her face, Varsha went on repeating the three words until she realized that Mr. Das and Mr. Iyer were also present there. However, in order to save Varsha from embarrassment, the two gentlemen diverted their gaze from the couple to the ceiling of the showroom, as if their eyes were their hearing organs.

'I had guessed that Saahil would be here,' Vaibhav announced as he entered the showroom just then.

'Why didn't you tell me then?' Varsha complained.

'You left the hostel before I could tell you. Saahil had told me earlier that he would buy the car today, so I didn't take you seriously when you said that he had gone missing. The alarm bells started ringing in my head after some time. Fearing that you might be correct, I came here searching for Saahil myself,' Vaibhav explained.

Saahil said, 'Anyway, everything is fine now. Let's celebrate the occasion. We will go to a nice restaurant in my new car.'

Mr. Das said, 'You people enjoy yourselves. I will have to go back to the library.' Mr. Iyer also had some important things to attend to. So he expressed his inability to go with them. Saahil paid the auto-rickshaw driver and asked Varsha and Vaibhav to wait for some time. After the formalities of the car purchase were completed, they headed for the restaurant.

On their way to the restaurant, Vaibhav asked Saahil to stop the car near an ATM as he needed to withdraw some cash. Varsha, who had skipped her dinner the previous night and her breakfast that morning, was hungry like a monster. She wanted to reach the restaurant as soon as possible. She asked Vaibhav, 'Can't you withdraw the money later?'

'No,' Vaibhav replied as he entered the ATM counter. Varsha followed him into the counter and asked him to hurry up.

Vaibhav pressed the 'cancel' button before inserting the card into the machine, and waited for the home screen to reappear. The delay annoyed Varsha. She asked, 'Why did you press the 'cancel' button even before inserting the card? People usually press the 'cancel' button after completing their transactions.'

'I do it both before and after doing any transaction,' Vaibhav said casually.

'Hello! This is an ATM, not a lavatory, where you flush the toilet before and after use. You are not going to contract any infection from the ATM,' Varsha said with clenched teeth.

'You never know. It's always better to be on the safe side.'

'You are horrible,' Varsha growled.

Vaibhav took his own sweet time to complete the transaction before they returned to the car.

As soon as they reached the restaurant, Varsha caught hold of the first waiter she could see, and asked, 'Is there something that you can serve right now – in a minute?'

'Yes, madam. Ice cream.'

'Good. Get me that immediately.'

'Which flavor, madam?'

'Any flavor will do. And don't bring only one or two scoops. Bring a large bowl full of ice cream.'

In no time, the waiter was back with a large bowl containing black currant ice cream. Saahil's eyes grew wide in surprise as Varsha devoured the whole bowl full of ice cream alone.

Saahil told Vaibhav, 'You see, she was on a hunger strike for a noble cause.'

The waiter sympathized with Varsha. 'In that case, she will find our "buffet lunch offer" very useful. We serve around thirty different items for just five hundred bucks, and you can eat as much as you want.' He emphasized on the last sentence.

While they were enjoying the buffet lunch, Varsha said, 'I am totally surprised. You never mentioned that you were going to buy the car so soon.'

Saahil said, 'After a few unsuccessful attempts, I realized that it was going to be a tough job to own a house. The comparatively easier task was to own a car. I thought it would be better to achieve at least one more target instead of going on wandering between targets. Mr. Iyer told me that I couldn't get a car loan because of my lack of documents, so the only option left was to pay the total price in lump sum and buy the car. I chose the cheapest car available. Mr. Iyer took pains to convince the owner of the showroom to sell me the car on a no-profit-no-loss basis. The owner didn't want to lose a good salesperson either. Still, the car costed me around three lakh rupees. I spent most of the money I had saved till now on this car, but it is worth it.'

'I can't wait to tell bhaiya that we have crossed one more hurdle. I think I have started liking the game that bhaiya has started,' Varsha smiled.

# Chapter 13

Two months passed by since Saahil bought the car. Only a month was left for the wedding to take place now. Two more obligations were yet to be fulfilled – a house and a bank balance of ten lakh rupees. Varsha and Saahil knew that it was impossible to fulfil these obligations in a month's time. Only a miracle could help them now. But unfortunately, miracles are a rare occurrence. The only thing they could rely on was *effort,* but even effort was not always capable of turning the impossible into possible. They had started feeling drained, physically and emotionally.

When they met in the evenings, they would sit with each other in utter silence for hours altogether. The stage of dreaming, enthusiasm, expectations, discussions and planning had passed long ago. They had come to the stage of practicality now. They were trying to live with the truth, and the sole truth in sight was that they wouldn't be able to marry each other. They couldn't bear to think of the day of Varsha's wedding with Alok when their lives would come to a standstill. After that day, they would be like zombies – living, but without life. They felt like death row prisoners waiting for the execution to be carried out.

Occasionally, Varsha would break the silence and say, 'Whatever happens, I will have no regrets. I am happy that I have chosen the right person for me. No one could have done what you have done for me in just a few months. What you have achieved is extraordinary. No one else could have achieved this much in such less time. I am so proud of you, and I love you. I will remain only yours wherever I go.'

Then they would kiss and sob, and sob and kiss until they got breathless.

One day, Varsha asked Mr. Dev directly, 'How can I marry someone who I don't love?'

Mr. Dev tried to convince her. 'People need not fall in love in order to marry. People need to marry so they can eventually fall in love one day.'

'That's absurd logic. No marriage can be successful without love.'

'Who says that love makes marriages successful? I think the word we are looking for is "habit". Married people are so accustomed to living with their partners that they can't even think of living without them.'

'Whatever. I am not going to marry anyone except Saahil. He will win the game and I will marry him. You just wait and watch.' Varsha found an unusual sternness in her own voice.

'Let's see who wins.'

'You will see,' Varsha tried to sound confident, but her inner self didn't support her voice much.

She entered her room, bolted the door and called Saahil. 'What are you doing, love?'

'Trying to figure out how I can buy a house within a month.' Saahil's tone sounded bland.

'Haven't you left hope yet?'

'I can't. The only thing that I have ever wanted desperately in my life is to have you. For me, losing hope means losing you, and I can't afford to lose you.'

'Please don't lose me. Take care, love.' Varsha ended the call as she was on the verge of crying. She didn't want Saahil to get weak and depressed because of her.

Before she could give in to crying, her phone rang. It was Makaan bhai on the other side.

'Hello, madam,' he started.

'Yes, Makaan bhai?'

'How serious is Mr. Saahil about buying a house?'

'As serious as he is about living,' Varsha replied.

'Then we should meet tomorrow. Can you come to my office?'

'We will be there.'

'I will wait.' Makaan bhai ended the call.

Varsha called Saahil up and asked him to be ready to meet Makaan bhai the next day.

When they met Makaan bhai the next day, he took them to the office of a builder who, according to Makaan bhai, was one of the richest and the most successful builders of the city. However, his office operated in a small room.

As they entered the office, Makaan bhai said 'hello' to the only person present there. The man, who was almost spherical in shape due to his huge bulk, rose from his chair with great difficulty and hugged Makaan bhai. 'Welcome, Makaan bhai. How is life going on?' The man had a big smile on his face.

'God's grace and well-wishes of friends like you have kept me fine, Mr. Seth.' Makaan bhai reciprocated Mr. Seth's smile, but he failed to reciprocate the hug as he could hardly encircle Mr. Seth's girth with his arms.

Mr. Seth invited them to sit. 'What would you like to have – tea or coffee?'

'Anything will do,' Makaan bhai replied.

'I will get special coffee for all of you in a minute.'

As Mr. Seth left the office, Saahil said to Makaan bhai, 'I think it will be better if we talk to the builder face-to-face instead of talking to his staff.'

'Mr. Seth himself is the builder,' Makaan bhai declared.

'What? You must be joking. He doesn't look rich from any aspect. His office is a small room. He doesn't have any staff in his office – not even a boy to get coffee for his visitors.'

'This is not his main office, and he doesn't keep any staff in this office since his doctor has advised him to do all the physical work himself. It's really essential for him to lose some weight.'

Mr. Seth was back with the coffee soon.

'You are very fast for your weight. Incredible.' Makaan bhai said, being really surprised.

'I always try to save two things – time and money, because time is money.' Mr. Seth laughed at his own lame joke.

Makaan bhai said, 'So now, let's save time and come to the point. This is Mr. Saahil. As I have already told you, he wants to own a house within a month from now, but he doesn't have money. He doesn't have the documents needed to get a loan either. Hence I have brought him to you. Please help him by any means.'

Mr. Seth said, 'Mr. Saahil, Makaan bhai and I discussed your matter yesterday. See, I am not going to help you.'

Saahil looked perplexed.

Mr. Seth continued, 'No, no. Don't misunderstand me. I mean to say that what I am going to offer you can't be called help. You may call it business. Let me explain. I have heard from Makaan bhai that you are a very efficient salesperson. He has told me how you have managed to rise against all odds in the last few months. You have gained Makaan bhai's confidence, and I believe Makaan bhai so I have decided to get into a deal with you. I want you to sell five 3-BHK houses from my new project which just got completed. In return, I will register a 1-BHK house in your favor as your commission. You won't have to pay anything for the house.'

Saahil wondered whether he should believe Mr. Seth or not. The commission he was offering was too much to believe.

Perhaps Mr. Seth sensed Saahil's suspicion. He said, 'I know what you are thinking. Why am I offering you such a big commission? Because I have established my business on human relations and I will be happy to add you to the list. I see a prospective successful agent in you. If this deal goes well, I will get many more customers through you in the future.'

'But I can't keep Varsha in a 1-BHK house,' Saahil said, concerned.

Varsha squeezed Saahil's hand. 'I can manage in a 1-BHK house. At this moment, what we need is a house. The number of rooms hardly matters. We can get a larger house in future when we have money. I think you should say yes to the proposal.'

'Women think more practically than men do,' Mr. Seth inferred.

'What if I fail to sell five houses?' Saahil asked.

'I won't register the house in your favor in that case, but I will pay you your commission in the form of money based on the number of houses you will have sold. So you won't lose anything,' Mr. Seth assured.

'But I have never been in the real estate business. I don't have any experience. It won't be possible for a newbie like me to sell five houses within a month.'

Makaan bhai interrupted, 'You don't need to worry. I am ready to help you with that. You only need to arrange the customers. I will be with you when you deal with the customers. I will help you at every step – starting from showing the houses to the customers to registration in their favor. Moreover, in order to make the task a bit easier for you still, I will arrange the first customer for you. So you have to arrange only four customers.'

Saahil looked at Makaan bhai. 'That means you will lose your commission for that house – the commission that you can avoid giving if you sell the house to the customer directly. Why would you suffer the loss?'

Makaan bhai said, 'We are businessmen, but that doesn't mean we judge everything in terms of profit and loss. I am able to enjoy my prosperity today because some people who valued humanity had helped me during the days of my poverty. Yesterday, they helped me. Today, I am helping you. Tomorrow, you may help someone else. That's how humanity survives through the ages.'

'That's really nice of you, but I can't accept the favor.'

'It's alright. I understand that your self-esteem doesn't allow you to accept the favor, but you can at least accept a debt,' said Makaan bhai.

Saahil gave Makaan bhai a quizzical look.

Makaan bhai explained, 'Consider my commission a debt. You can pay me the amount when you have the money in future.'

Saahil thought over it and said, 'Yes, that can be done. Still, I don't think I can even arrange a single customer. I am not feeling confident.'

Varsha said, 'I know you can complete the task. Your determination and perseverance are extraordinary. A few months ago, you were a salesperson with a small salary. Your hard work made you a man of success in a matter of just months. You persevered till now despite all odds. Now, we are very close to getting success. A little more effort and we can be together forever. Please don't lose hope at this crucial stage. You yourself had said yesterday that losing hope was like losing me. Please don't let go of this opportunity.' Her eyes were wet.

Saahil sat silently for a few minutes. He wasn't left with any more energy. His enthusiasm had died down. He didn't want to lose hope, but hope wasn't ready to be with him anymore.

He looked at everyone and said, 'I am thankful to all of you for being so nice to me, but I don't think I am capable of completing the task. I can't accept Mr. Seth's offer. I am sorry.' He rose from his chair and left the office quite unexpectedly.

With a heavy heart, Varsha apologized to Makaan bhai and Mr. Seth for having wasted their time. Mr. Seth said, 'Madam, never mind the waste of time, but I am really sorry about Mr. Saahil's decision. Sometimes, decisions matter more than deeds. One wrong decision can change one's life completely. Anyway, please tell Mr. Saahil that the offer is still open. He will be welcome if he changes his mind any time. I will be happy to work with him.'

# Chapter 14

Winter set in a bit early that year. Vaibhav's belongings like his suitcase, his bag, his books, his shoes, all of which were usually kept under his bed had found their place on his bed. And Vaibhav, who usually slept on his bed during the warmer seasons of the year, had found his place under his bed since the onset of winter. He was of the opinion that the bed base worked like another roof (beside that of the room) and provided some more protection from the cold. He had not yet found a solution to the cold floor on which he slept though.

Vaibhav was lying under his bed after dinner, a mattress beneath him and the thickest possible quilt above him. Saahil was lying on his bed, looking at the ceiling which was full of cobwebs. He mused philosophically, 'Everything has changed so much.'

Vaibhav peeped from under his bed, followed Saahil's gaze and agreed, 'You are right. The cobwebs around the ceiling fan were not there earlier.'

'I am not talking of that change.'

Vaibhav thought for a moment and said, 'Something else has changed too. Our maid, Sakku *bai,* has not been buying pumpkins for her son, Munna, lately. These days, she quotes the price of cauliflower instead of pumpkin while asking for a salary hike.'

'Can you ever talk sense? I am not talking of these petty changes. I am talking of life. Life was without worries till a few months ago. In those days, I was a carefree boy, though I hardly had any money. Today, I earn a lot, but I am not happy. I am always worried about Varsha. Till a few months ago, she was a happy-go-lucky girl who lived life to the fullest. But now...she rarely smiles these days, and it's all because of me. I have filled her life with sorrow and worries. It would have been better if I had not come into her life at all.'

Vaibhav emerged from under his bed and took a seat beside Saahil. 'We all go through difficult times, but the good thing is that difficult times do not last forever. You should spend more time with Varsha. That will keep both of you happy.'

'On the contrary, I have started staying away from her as much as possible. She must learn to stay away from me and get used to living without me. That will help when she gets married to Alok and goes away from me to stay with him.'

'Don't be so negative. She will never go away from you. She is only yours.'

'I have had enough of that daydream. Varsha and I must accept the reality. One more thing - you should start searching for a new roommate. I will leave this hostel and this city after Varsha's wedding. Every place in this city will remind me of her. I won't be able to live in this city without her.'

'I won't stay in this room without you. If you move away, I will also move into my parents' place. For quite some time, my father has been asking me to look after his business, but you won't need to leave this city. You will leave this hostel and move into your new house to start a new life with Varsha. You people will be with each other forever. Don't worry.' Vaibhav smiled confidently.

Saahil smiled mechanically.

Varsha smiled illogically, before she realized that there was no reason to smile. She was sitting alone in her room. A smile in the absence of any activity, any conversation and any thought was definitely illogical. She wondered if she was going mad. The very thought frightened her.

She thought of calling Saahil, but discarded the idea the very next moment, not wanting to bother him with such petty things. She considered giving him more space as she had seen him avoiding her lately.

It was only a matter of a month now. She couldn't stop thinking that if Saahil failed, she would be damned to live with an unknown species (she couldn't find a more appropriate designation for Alok) in an unknown world. She would be away from Saahil. She would be away from her brother. The thought frightened her even more. She would do anything to be with Saahil. But what could she do?

Aryan, her pet dog, wriggled through the partially open door of her room and cuddled up next to her feet. Varsha caressed its head affectionately. Aryan reminded her of Naina who was once hell-bent on marrying Aryan because a saint living in the Himalayas had advised her to do so. Varsha smiled as she remembered the incident.

The very next moment, something occurred to her. She called Naina, but Naina didn't respond. Varsha called again. Naina still didn't receive the call. Varsha tried a third time.

Naina answered this time. 'Hello. What's up?'

Varsha asked, 'Why didn't you receive my calls earlier?'

'My numerologist has said that three is my lucky number for today. So I was waiting for your third call.'

Varsha sighed. Thanks to the numerologist, Naina's lucky number was not ten, she thought. Varsha said, 'I need your help.'

'Yes, tell me.'

'You often talk about a saint living in the Himalayas — the saint who advised you to marry a dog. Do you remember?'

'Of course, yes. I often visit him. He now lives in a village near our city.'

'That's wonderful. Can you take me to him?'

'Yes, we will go some day.'

'No, we will go tomorrow.'

'But tomorrow...'

'Please, please, please. I don't have much time in hand. It's the matter of my life.'

'Alright, we will go tomorrow. But why do you need to visit him?'

'I will tell you on the way. Bye.'

'Bye.'

Varsha and Naina set out on their journey to meet the saint the next morning. Though it was a journey of only fifty kilometers, the jerky ride along the uneven, muddy country road made the journey seem endless.

On the way, Varsha asked, 'Did the saint's advice about your wedding work? Did you marry a dog? Did the dog die? Can you marry your boyfriend now?'

'I married the dog. The dog died. But my boyfriend refused to marry me after.'

'Why?'

'He said he didn't want to marry a dog's widow.'

Varsha suppressed a bout of laughter. 'Oh! I am very sorry to hear that, but don't worry. There must be someone better waiting for you.'

'I don't think so anymore. I fell in love thrice after that and I had to break-up each time.' Naina looked sad.

This time, Varsha didn't find it funny. She genuinely felt sorry for Naina.

Naina continued, 'Now, I am afraid to get into a relationship because I think I am not good enough to let a relationship last long.'

Had it been some other occasion, Varsha would have advised Naina to not be so skeptical and superstitious about everything, for it was this quality of hers that had driven her boyfriends away. But today, Varsha refrained from saying so because she herself was in a desperate need to try anything, even that which one might consider superstitious, in order to marry Saahil. That's why she had set out on this journey in the first place.

Naina broke the silence again. 'By the way, why do you need to meet the saint?'

Varsha said, 'You know about Saahil and me.'

'Yes, I heard that your brother set some impossible targets for Saahil to achieve.'

'True. Saahil tried his best to achieve most of those targets, though it was beyond the capacity of any man to do so. But now, there is no hope left. Only some miracle can help us now. So I thought the saint might do something for us.'

'I thought you never had faith in such things.'

'Despair makes people do the unthinkable. I am ready to do anything in order to continue to have Saahil in my life.' The tears that Varsha tried to hold back in her eyes made her vision blurred. Through the layers of tears in her eyes, she could see the hazy outline of a bunch of huts at a distance.

'We are almost there,' Naina said.

As they parked their car outside the fence surrounding the huts, Naina said, 'We have to leave our cell phones in the car. They are not allowed inside the campus of the hermitage.'

Upon entering the campus, Naina paid the entry fee of one thousand bucks at the reception desk.

The receptionist said, 'Madam, the entry fee is one thousand bucks per person.'

Naina took out a card from her purse. 'I have got a lifetime-membership card. The money I gave you was her entry fee,' she said, pointing towards Varsha.

The receptionist apologized, 'Oh! I didn't know that.'

'What? They even offer lifetime membership?' Varsha asked Naina.

Instead of allowing Naina to reply, the receptionist spoke, 'Yes, madam, we offer lifetime membership, which is very cost-effective – pay only once and enjoy our services for as long as you are alive. We provide solutions to all types of problems like business related matters, marriage related issues, ghost problems, etcetera. Alternatively, you may avail our annual pack offer.'

'They seem quite professional,' Varsha thought.

The receptionist continued, 'We have got the use-and-throw pack for one time users.'

'Use-and-throw pack? What's that?' Varsha asked.

'You *use* our services and we *throw* your problems away from you. You pay only once and we provide the service only once. Besides, we have got the twin pack for couples, the friendship pack for groups, and the unlimited pack for frequent users,' the receptionist added with a smile.

Varsha whispered to Naina, 'He sounds like the salesperson of some internet service provider. Are you sure we have come to the right place?'

'Shut up,' Naina hissed.

Naina had already got a lifetime membership card, so Varsha appeared to be the only prospective client. The receptionist asked her, 'Which pack would you like to go for?'

'The use-and-throw pack,' Naina answered on behalf of Varsha.

The receptionist took ten thousand rupees from Varsha upfront and issued them the receipt for the use-and-throw pack. He then gave them a token bearing a serial number and asked them to wait.

As they proceeded to the waiting area, Varsha asked Naina, 'Don't you think their services are quite costly?'

'Not costlier than the lives of people they serve,' Naina replied.

Varsha kept quiet, though she was not convinced. She didn't want to argue with a fan who had registered for a lifetime membership.

They waited in the waiting area which was nothing but a large garden. All the people waiting there had one feature in common – they all looked rich, but grief-stricken and tense. After they had waited for about two hours, a man in white clothes called out their serial number.

The man led them into a huge hut where a number of workers in white clothes sat on a large carpet spread on the floor. The clients sitting in front of each of them were trying to describe their problems as accurately as possible, with the help of occasional melodrama that attracted others' attention too. The workers were busy jotting down the clients' problems, taking special care to include some part of the melodrama in their notes. The intensity of the melodrama indicated the severity of the problem perhaps, and the severity of the problem decided the amount of money the client had to pay in order to get the solution.

The person accompanying Varsha and Naina introduced them to one of the workers who was unoccupied at the time, and said, 'You may describe your problem to him. He will note it down and the piece of paper will be given to the saint before you meet him.'

They sat before him and Varsha told him why she was there and what she wanted from the saint. The worker jotted down everything in brief and sent the paper to the saint's room. After a while, he said to Varsha, 'Now, you may go inside, but alone.'

Varsha objected, 'No. I want my friend to accompany me.'

Naina tried to convince her. 'It's the rule here. You have to go alone to meet the saint. There is nothing to worry.'

The worker said, 'Madam, it's all about faith. If you don't have faith in the saint, you won't achieve anything by meeting him.'

Naina patted Varsha on the back. 'Before entering the saint's room, leave all your doubts outside.'

'And your purse too,' the worker added.

Varsha reminded herself, 'I am ready to do anything in order to be with Saahil.' She handed her purse to Naina and entered the saint's room hesitantly. The saint sat there on a sofa, with his head bent over the piece of paper that described Varsha's problem. She couldn't see his face yet, so she simply greeted him with folded hands.

'God bless you. Take a seat,' replied the saint, still engrossed in the matter written on the piece of paper in his hand.

Varsha sat before him, but as soon as the saint sat back in the sofa and they looked at each other, they were shocked.

After a momentary silence, Varsha said, 'No, I don't believe this.'

'Even I don't want you to believe it,' the saint replied as he tossed the piece of paper into the wastepaper basket. 'I must admit that I can't perform any miracle to solve your problem. I must confess, at least before you, that I am no saint. Please take your money back and go away. Go away at once. Please.' He put his palms over his face.

Varsha's dreams and expectations got shattered once again. She couldn't move from her seat. She wanted to be angry at the saint. He had no right to try to cheat her. But she couldn't get mad at him. He looked more helpless than she herself was. Nonetheless, he owed her an explanation. She asked, 'Amit bhaiya, why do you do all this?'

Amit, the saint, was an old friend of Mr. Dev. He replied, 'You have always been like a younger sister to me. I won't hide anything from you. Everyone is not lucky enough to get a job or be wealthy enough to start a business. After the completion of my graduation, I spent my time pursuing two things – a job-hunt and my hobby. My hobby was to study people – their emotions, thoughts, intentions. It's quite an odd hobby, and also a useless one, you might remark. But it was not quite so. As I pursued my hobby, I gradually developed expertise in the matter, so much so that I could guess people's emotions almost correctly just by observing their body language. I could even tell about their past to some extent just by guesswork.'

'Don't you ever get it wrong about the matters of the past?' Varsha got curious. She forgot her own problem for a moment.

'Almost never. There is a golden rule. I always make generalized statements, statements that hold true in almost everyone's life. I mostly say things related to negative emotions because people like to hold their negative emotions close to themselves. I make statements like *you have lost someone dear to you in the past* or *you had never wanted your life to be what it is today* or *you always repent a wrong decision you took in the past.*'

'The whole thing sounds like some kind of science.' Varsha's amazement was evident. 'And what about the statements about future?'

'The rule remains the same: always generalize it. After a few days, I learned a few magic tricks from a magician friend of mine. That's all about how I became a so called saint. You see, my hobby finally helped me and my staff to earn our bread and butter.'

'What did you do in the Himalayas?'

'I have never been to the Himalayas in my life. As you know, a degree or a certificate from a foreign university carries extra importance in many professions. Things are not so different in my profession either. The story that I have gained special powers by meditating in the Himalayas added to the credibility of my profession.'

'Don't you ever feel guilty about cheating people?'

'Initially, I didn't. I was quite happy. But my conscience started biting me soon, so much so that I started spending sleepless nights. Earlier, my sole motive was to cheat and earn, but I gradually started realizing people's pain as I listened to their problems every day. I developed a sympathetic and genuine attitude towards solving their problems. These days, I analyze their psyche and motivate and teach them to be happy. We donate most of the money we earn to orphanages, hospitals, and charitable organizations. We don't spend any money on our luxury. My staff and I live a very simple life. We dedicate two days in a week to solve the problems of the poor without charging them anything. To be very frank, I don't feel guilty anymore.'

'And what do you have to say about what you did to Naina?' Varsha asked.

'Naina?'

'Naina, my friend. You asked her to marry a dog. She is a blind believer of yours. She followed your advice blindly, and her boyfriend has now refused to marry her.'

'Yes, I remember.'

'Is that how you help people?'

'I didn't intend to help her. I helped her boyfriend instead.'

'What?'

'When I met her boyfriend and her separately, I found out that her boyfriend was completely fed up with their relationship because of her skeptic and superstitious nature. I advised Naina to change her attitude many a times, but she didn't care. Their relationship was suffocating her boyfriend. He desperately wanted to get out of the relationship, but she would just not leave him, no matter what. He needed a reason to break up with her, and I gave him the reason. I advised her to marry a dog, and advised her boyfriend to break up with her by giving her the reason that he didn't want to marry a dog's widow. Both Naina and her boyfriend needed help. I helped the one who was more helpless.' After a pause, Amit continued, 'Can I expect you to keep my secrets?'

Varsha nodded with a subtle smile on her face. 'I will. You are not that bad after all. Anyway, I have to leave now. I need to find out the solution to my problem.'

'Wait a minute.' Amit pulled out a drawer in his table. It contained money. 'Take back the amount you deposited at the reception. One more thing – I can't perform any miracle for you, but I would certainly like to help you. Should I talk to Dev? I can try to convince him to change his decision.'

'That will be of no avail. He won't listen to anyone. He has been quite stubborn in this matter.'

Amit thought for a while and said, 'In that case, can you come back with your boyfriend tomorrow. I will see what I can do.'

'I will try,' Varsha said and left.

After much effort, Varsha was able to convince Saahil to come meet Amit.

The next day when they met Amit, he tried to soothe Saahil. 'Make yourself comfortable. I am like your elder brother. Don't think that I am some saint who is going to perform some ritual to solve your problem. I just want to discuss your problem with you and try to help you find a solution. Varsha has already informed me about your problem. She has also informed me that you have persevered against all odds till now and have achieved the unachievable. Why are you backing out at this crucial stage?'

Saahil sighed. 'I don't see any hope. Everything is going wrong in my life.'

Amit said, 'It's always too early to arrive at the conclusion that things are going wrong in your life. Let me tell you a story.

There was a man, very rich and very fond of food. He always complained to God, "Everything is wrong. You gave me two hands, two legs, two eyes and two ears. Then why did you give me only one mouth and one stomach? Had you given me two mouths and two stomachs, I could have enjoyed eating more."

'God replied, "I have designed everything carefully. The parts that you need to work are more in number so that you can earn more bread and butter for your family and yourself. On the other hand, the parts that are meant to consume the bread and butter are less in number so that you need less resources to satisfy your needs."

'But that made no difference to the man's psychology. He would still complain, "Everything is wrong. You should have given me two mouths and two stomachs."

'The man went on devouring all the food he could get his hands on, no matter whether he needed them or not. He continued putting on weight till his body looked like a huge ball. He couldn't perform his daily activities anymore. He couldn't even breathe properly. He developed a number of ailments. Finally, his doctor told him that he must stop eating voraciously if he wanted to live.

'Given his love of food, the task was absolutely difficult for him. Nevertheless, his life was also dear to him. The man began dieting, but it was very difficult for him to overcome his gluttony. He complained to God again, "Everything is wrong. Why have you given me this stomach and this mouth? All my problems are due to them. Had you not given me these two things, I wouldn't have eaten anything at all, I wouldn't have been so fat, I would have been a healthy man without any ailments."

'God said, "You complained earlier. You are complaining now. Then tell me – was it wrong then or is it wrong now?"

'The man didn't know what to say. He remained silent.

'God said, "It wasn't wrong then. It isn't wrong now. The only things that are wrong are your perception and your actions. I always decide the best for you. Your perception and your actions make things wrong or right for you."

'So you see, things may seem wrong now, but they may not remain so in the future. Hence, there is nothing to harass yourself with. If things seem wrong, you must try to make them right.'

Saahil hadn't thought that he would ever listen to a saint's words so attentively. But to his own surprise, he had. The saint's words were capable enough to cause a surge of optimism in him and he could feel it, but he still had doubts. 'However hard I try, I won't succeed because of the lack of time.'

'Don't try to decide the fate of your future by yourself. Let future decide your fate. You can only try,' Amit said. 'If you try, you may succeed or you may fail. But if you don't try, there will be only one result – failure. Moreover, you won't lose anything by trying.'

Saahil sat silent for a moment, then nodded. 'I will try.'

# Chapter 15

Saahil and Varsha left Amit's hermitage in the afternoon. By the time they reached the city, the sun had retired after the day's hard work. Though it could shut its office early in the winter season, it had to work extra hard throughout the day, fighting with the mist and cold – no easy task, certainly – but not tougher than the task that Saahil had decided to take on.

As soon as he reached the city, Saahil called up Makaan bhai. 'Is Mr. Seth's offer still open for me? Can you take me to him?' he asked him.

Makaan bhai replied, 'He is not a person who changes his mind frequently, and he will be happy to know that you have changed your mind. My offer is also still open – I will get you one customer. You will only have to arrange for four more. Plus, I will help you at every step. We will go to Mr. Seth's office tomorrow. From there, we will proceed to the project site. I will show you the houses and tell you all the details of the project.'

'Thank you.' Saahil cut the call and looked at Varsha. 'I was stupid. I had thought that I was making things easier for you by avoiding you and making you get used to living without me. I didn't know that I was actually making things more difficult for both of us. I had forgotten that you are my strength and inspiration. From now on, I want you to be with me most of the time.'

Varsha smiled. 'That goes without saying. I will always be with you – I am like your bones.'

Saahil corrected her. 'You mean, you are like my soul, right?'

'No. I mean, I am like your bones. Your soul will leave you after your death. But I will always be with you, even after your death.'

'That's…that's scientifically romantic.' Saahil gave her a confused smile.

The next day, Makaan bhai and Saahil met Mr. Seth at his office again. Mr. Seth explained some details of the project to Saahil. Then, he asked Makaan bhai, 'Do I need to accompany you to the project site?'

'No. You don't have to bother over it. Leave everything to me,' replied Makaan bhai.

After visiting the project site and understanding all the details of the project from Makaan bhai, Saahil went to meet Varsha in the afternoon.

'So, what do you think about the project?' Varsha asked.

Saahil replied, 'I am not an expert in real estate, but I can say one thing – Mr. Seth doesn't cheat his customers. He has used materials of good quality. The prices are affordable. I think if I get eager customers, it won't be very difficult for me to convince them to buy the houses. The only problem is that it's difficult to get such customers in so less time.'

Varsha thought a moment and said, 'Don't worry. Let's go for division of labor.'

'How?'

'I will try to get one customer. Makaan bhai has already promised that he will get one customer for you. We can ask Vaibhav to try to get a customer. So then, you will have to arrange only two more customers.'

'Vaibhav? Vaibhav is the most inefficient person on earth.'

'Don't underestimate his efficiency. He remains in touch with people and is well connected. Don't forget that he was the one who arranged our first meeting.'

When they talked about the same with Vaibhav, he said, 'You are asking me to arrange only one customer? You should ask for more. You know what I am capable of.'

'I know what you are capable of, that's why I am asking you to arrange only one customer. In fact, I know that even that is not possible for you. It's Varsha who has confidence in you, and you have got less than a month's time to prove her right,' Saahil retorted.

'A month! You must be kidding. Two days.' Vaibhav waved two fingers before Saahil's face. 'In two days, I will stand in front of you with your first customer.'

'Don't you ever get tired of boasting?' Saahil asked irritatedly.

'I have got so many good qualities, you know. The best among them is that I never boast.'

Varsha smiled. 'Yes, we can see that.'

It took Vaibhav only one day, however, to prove Saahil wrong. He reached Saahil's office the next day with a young man in his early thirties. Vaibhav whispered to Saahil, 'I kept my promise. Here is Roopesh, your first customer.'

Saahil shook hands with Roopesh whose hands were covered in a pair of latex gloves. The lower half of his face was covered by a surgical mask. Guessing that Roopesh must be a doctor, Saahil said, 'Doctor, you forgot to remove your gloves and mask.'

Roopesh said, 'You guessed it wrong. I am not a doctor. Studies show that we transmit a lot of infections to each other by touch and breath. That's why I wear gloves and a mask.'

'Oh! Very healthy habit, I must say,' Saahil complimented him.

When Saahil offered him a chair to sit, he took out a bottle of disinfectant solution from his pocket, sprayed it on the chair and sat down, taking utmost care not to touch too many other things in the office.

Saahil told him all the features of the 3-BHK house and asked, 'Would you like to see the house today?'

'Undoubtedly. I have read somewhere that an average man postpones half his important tasks for the future, and I don't want to be an average man. Let's go right now,' replied Roopesh.

'Very well, sir.'

Upon reaching the project site, Saahil said, 'Mr. Roopesh, the house on the corner plot is still available. It will cost you a bit more, but a house on a corner plot has got some advantages. Would you like to see it?'

'No, I don't want it. I would prefer to have a house that has got other houses adjacent to it on both sides.'

'Is there any particular reason for it, sir?'

'Men living in such houses grow rich early.'

'You must have read it somewhere, I am sure,' Saahil said.

'No, I haven't. I have written it in my book. I am writing a book on '*Lifestyle in relation to the location of houses*'.'

'The concept is quite unique, I must say.' Saahil tried to flatter him. 'Sir, is there any logic behind what you said? Why do men living in such houses grow rich early?'

Roopesh explained, 'When you live in such a house, you have more families in your vicinity, in comparison to a house on a corner plot. This way, your wife finds more luxury elements like cars, refrigerators, furniture in your neighbors' houses for comparison. The more she compares, the more she places her demands before you to buy elements more luxurious than those in the neighbors' houses. The more she demands, the more you need to earn to fulfil those demands. So, you work more and earn more. As a result, you grow rich.'

'Highly commendable observation, indeed,' Saahil praised Roopesh. Saahil knew by this time that Vaibhav had brought with him a clone of him. He didn't mind tolerating another Vaibhav as long as it helped him achieve his target. He showed him the house, explaining each and every detail of it. Then, he asked, 'Sir, what have you decided? Would you like to go for it?'

'Definitely. The house is good. The price is affordable. Moreover, I trust Vaibhav. Hence, I can go for it blindly.'

Still unable to believe that he had actually got his first customer so easily, Saahil hesitantly asked, 'So when should we go for the deal?'

'What do you mean by "when"? Can't we start the process today itself? I told you, I don't like to postpone important tasks to future dates.'

'Very well, sir,' Saahil replied. He called up Makaan bhai and Mr. Seth, and arranged their meeting with Roopesh. That very afternoon, Roopesh paid the booking amount for the house.

After Roopesh had left, Mr. Seth said to Saahil, 'You are going really fast. Good.'

'It all happened because of Vaibhav,' Saahil said.

'You are lucky to have a friend like him.'

Varsha said the same thing to Saahil when they met that evening. 'Vaibhav was right. You should have asked him for more.'

Saahil said, 'Don't get inflated ideas about his capability. He was able to convince Mr. Roopesh only because both of them belong to the same species.'

'What?'

'Nothing. You won't understand.'

'You should at least thank Vaibhav.'

'Why should I?'

'He helped you so much.'

'What's the big deal? That's what friends are for. Moreover, friendship and formality can never flourish together.'

Saahil went on searching for more customers. Meanwhile, Makaan bhai kept his promise and arranged a customer for Saahil. Even Varsha didn't fail to keep her promise. She told all her friends about this property, and it turned out that the father of one of her friends was looking to purchase a house at that time. After Varsha and Saahil had shown him the house and he checked all the documents, he agreed to go for it.

Only two weeks were left before the wedding now, but neither Varsha nor Saahil was depressed anymore. It wasn't because they had found a supernatural confident about them getting married to each other, but because the customer-hunt didn't allow them any time to get depressed. They approached everyone who seemed like a prospective buyer. Every day, Saahil would take a number of prospective buyers to the project site in his car. He would offer them soft drinks and show them around the houses, but none of them seemed inclined to buy.

He encountered various types of people in the process. There were the *window-shoppers* whose favorite pastime was to enjoy free rides in the air-conditioned cars of real estate agents and oblige them by pseudo-reluctantly accepting the soft drink offered. There were the *soothsayers* who could foresee the dark future of the property with regard to the half-lives of the materials used and the possibility of acquisition of the land by the government. Then there were the *time travellers* who preferred to travel two decades back into the past when it came to the price of the property.

Saahil was running short of time. He discussed the problem with Makaan bhai. 'I am trying my best, but I am not able to convince any of my customers to buy a house. I don't know what to do.'

Makaan bhai said, 'I had told you that I would be with you when you showed the houses to customers. Why didn't you call me when you took them to the site?'

'You have already done so much for me and I have already wasted a lot of your time. I didn't want to waste your time anymore, so I went on to show them the houses myself.'

'Why are you so modest? It's not good to be modest all the time. You should have called me. We salespersons need only one thing to invest in our business – time and I have a lot of it. Now, call all the customers once more and tell them that we have got some more properties to show them. I will accompany you this time.'

'You mean, some other properties that belong to Mr. Seth?'

'No. These properties belong to some other builders I work with.'

'Why should we show the customers the properties that do not belong to Mr. Seth? Even if they buy them, it won't help me achieve my target of selling five houses from Mr. Seth's project,' Saahil objected.

'Have faith in me. Please do as I say,' Makaan bhai tried to assure him.

'I believe you. I will call them today itself,' Saahil said, but he was not entirely convinced. He became suspicious of Makaan bhai's intentions and wondered if he wanted to snatch his customers. Only the next moment, he remembered that Makaan bhai had himself given him a customer of his. Saahil felt guilty for suspecting Makaan bhai's intentions. Moreover, he wasn't left with many options. He had already tried and failed to sell the houses himself, so he decided to follow Makaan bhai's advice.

He called up all the prospective buyers once more and fixed appointments with the willing ones. He made sure to accommodate all of them in the next two days. He had never valued time so much in his life before. When he informed Makaan bhai about the arrangement, he cancelled all his own appointments for the next two days so he could be with Saahil all the time.

This time, they showed the customers some properties that belonged to other builders. Makaan bhai took the lead and explained the details of the houses to them, but none of the properties were up to the mark. Some of them were not even free from litigation, as told to the customers by Makaan bhai. He added, 'Sir, it's my duty to reveal everything about the property to you before you decide to buy it.' Some of the properties were very highly priced. Some were not move-in ready. Some houses had been built using substandard materials.

As a result, all the customers ended up dissatisfied and asked, 'Can't you show us something that's worth buying?'

Makaan bhai would then think for a moment and recall, 'Yes, there is one more project.' Saahil and he would take them to Mr. Seth's project. 'Sir, this move-in ready project is free from litigations. The price is affordable too. The materials used are also good, but this project should be your last choice. The ones we showed you earlier may be high-priced, but they are better. You should consider buying one of those.'

The customers would think, 'Oh! Sure. You must be getting more commission by selling the high-priced houses. Why shouldn't one buy one of these affordable houses instead?' They would say, 'Mr. Saahil has already showed us these houses.'

Makaan bhai would then apologize. 'Oh! I didn't know that. Anyway, that's all we have. Sir, we would appreciate if you make a decision quickly because the houses on this project are getting sold very quickly. I don't know why people are after these cheap houses so much.'

This process went on for two days. Saahil asked Makaan bhai, 'Now what?'

'Now, wait for two more days patiently, then call them and ask them what they have decided.'

It was not easy for Saahil to keep his patience. The ongoing wedding preparations were making him even more impatient. Mr. Dev was on the verge of winning the game. The owner of a prosperous hotel chain didn't need to go searching for a venue for the wedding. No wonder, making arrangements for the wedding and the reception was a cakewalk for him. Varsha mostly tried to stay out of her house in order to avoid witnessing the wedding preparations, which depressed her.

After having waited impatiently for two days, Saahil called up the customers and asked them what they had decided.

The first customer shouted from the other end, 'Bad network. I can't hear anything. Hello...hello...hello...' Then the line was cut. The (voluntary) bad network interfered every time Saahil tried to speak to him.

The second customer simply replied, 'I am very busy. We will talk next month.'

The third customer said, 'Wrong number.'

Receiving such evading responses was not new for Saahil. He went ahead and called the other customers. Two of them had developed serious health problems, and had been advised absolute physical and mental rest. One customer had postponed his plan of buying a house.

Only three more customers remained to be called. Bored and frustrated of listening to the same lame excuses, he decided to play a game with himself. He decided that if he received another lame excuse for not buying a house, he would win. And if the customer's response was positive, he would lose. No doubt, he would be extremely happy to lose.

He called the next customer, feeling sure that he would win. But no, he didn't. To his surprise, he lost. Yes, he lost the game, and it was the first time in his life when he felt so happy to have lost a game.

He called the next one and yes! He was defeated by this customer too. He couldn't believe that he had suffered two consecutive defeats. With this defeat, he had achieved the target of giving five customers (including those provided by Makaan bhai, Vaibhav and Varsha) to Mr. Seth.

He called up the last customer, and it was a tie. However, Saahil didn't mind it so much anymore.

He informed Makaan bhai and Mr. Seth about the success. They were both really happy for him. They convinced the customers to pay the booking amount as soon as possible. The customers obliged.

Saahil asked Makaan bhai, 'These two customers showed no interest in Mr. Seth's project when I showed them the property, but they changed their mind after you accompanied me to the project site to show them the houses. What was the reason? I know you did something extra. What was it?'

Makaan bhai smiled. 'I talked to them in a language that all customers understand.'

'Which language?'

'The language of *comparison*.'

Saahil looked confused.

Makaan bhai explained, 'Have you ever noticed the one thing that all customers do before buying something?' He himself answered, 'They *compare*. No customer buys anything without comparing it with the others of its kind. Sometimes, people realize the worth of something only when they compare it with the others of its kind, and find it better than them. We knew that Mr. Seth's project was worth buying, but the customers didn't believe it when you showed them only Mr. Seth's project. When we showed them the other projects that had some shortcomings, they realized the true worth of

Mr. Seth's project. I advised them to buy one of the costly houses instead of buying one from Mr. Seth's project because I didn't want to seem to favor Mr. Seth's project. We occasionally need to do such things to convince the customers.' Makaan bhai winked and smiled.

Saahil hesitantly asked, 'But doesn't it seem unethical?'

'Not when I am sure that I am not cheating my customers, and am giving them the best.'

As soon as the customers paid the booking amount, Mr. Seth kept his promise and initiated the process of registering a 1-BHK house in Saahil's favor. Owing to Mr. Seth's contacts, things happened so fast that Saahil had to try hard to believe that he was the owner of his own house now. It was equally difficult for him to believe that he had crossed one more hurdle set by Mr. Dev.

# Chapter 16

'I own a house now. I am supposed to be happy. Perhaps, I am happy. But my happiness has been adulterated by the sorrow of our uncertain destiny. Why does happiness always come in such an impure form?' Saahil asked.

'Some things are more beautiful when they are impure. Even gold is of little use in its purest form,' Varsha tried to console Saahil as she held his hand more tightly.

They sat by the river bank, staring at the hazy horizon where the narcissistic moonlit sky was kissing its own reflection in the river. For Saahil and Varsha, everything was as hazy as the horizon. With only four days left before the wedding and one more impossible target to be achieved, their future looked blurred. They knew that getting a balance of ten lakh rupees in Saahil's bank account within four days was just impossible. All their emotions – love, hope, desperation, anxiety, sorrow – in conflict with one another had given way to a certain numbness, like all the colors of the rainbow mixing up to produce a pure white.

Varsha was fidgeting with the buttons on Saahil's shirt. 'Hey, we haven't yet shopped for the clothes that you would wear at our wedding,' she said, stressing the last two words. 'Let's go shopping tomorrow.'

'Yes, we will,' Saahil agreed at once.

Varsha had been skeptical about Saahil's willingness to go, since their chances of getting married seemed slim. 'I hadn't expected you to agree so quickly.'

'I would love to do anything that would keep me in your company during these four days. I want to live the last four days of my life with you.'

'What do you mean by the last four days of your life? You are not thinking of suicide, right?' Varsha got worried and sat up straight.

'Certainly not. But for me, life is synonymous with you. If you go away from my life, the word 'life' will vanish from my dictionary.'

Varsha hugged Saahil tightly. She lacked the words to console Saahil. She let the hug do the consoling.

The next morning, Saahil parked his car near Varsha's house and waited for her to go shopping. Meanwhile, he strolled over to the adjoining hotel that belonged to Mr. Dev. The wedding preparations going on at the hotel were evident, even from the outside. Bright and colorful chandeliers, elegant furniture, and rich floral decorations marked the lavishness of the upcoming event. Saahil had heard from Varsha that no bookings had been allowed for the hotel for the next week in order to keep the rooms unoccupied for the guests who would attend the wedding. It was evident from the array of luxury cars parked in the parking lot of the hotel that the guests had already started arriving for the wedding. The elegant attire of the guests made them look like celebrities. The whole scenario gave Saahil a complex. He was convinced for a moment that he was ineligible to marry Varsha. He couldn't bear the sight anymore. It was quite painful for him. He returned to his car.

He suddenly recalled that a couple of years ago, while playing cricket, the ball had hit Vaibhav in the testicles. He had rolled on the ground in pain.

Saahil had expressed his concern asking, 'Is it very painful?'

Vaibhav had shrieked in pain, 'It's as painful as seeing your girlfriend marry someone else.'

Saahil had laughed a lot that day. But now, he understood that Vaibhav was indeed correct. Seeing one's girlfriend marry someone else was as painful as getting one's testicles hit by a cricket ball.

While Saahil was engrossed in his thoughts, Varsha arrived to occupy the seat beside him in his car. 'What are you thinking?' she asked, trying to smile.

'It's quite painful,' Saahil said.

'What's painful?'

'Seeing you about to marry someone else,' Saahil replied.

The smile on Varsha's lips vanished.

Saahil continued, 'It's as painful as getting one's testicles hit by a cricket ball.'

'What?' This time, Varsha burst into laughter. 'Sometimes, I find you so funny.' She kissed him on the lips.

Saahil looked at Varsha in shock. 'What are you doing? We are just outside your house. What if someone sees you kissing me?'

'I will be very happy. Everyone will come to know that you are my love, and Alok will call off the wedding.'

'Not a bad idea.' This time, Saahil kissed Varsha on the lips. Both laughed.

They spent the whole day shopping. However, Varsha didn't behave like the usual aggressive-shopper-girl she was. Saahil noticed that she willingly chose things quickly so that she could spend less time with the salespersons and more time with him.

All that Saahil did the whole day was stare at Varsha like he was seeing her for the *last* time. He was least bothered about the wedding clothes that Varsha was purchasing for him. Every time Varsha chose something for him and asked for his opinion, he simply said, 'Anything you like.'

Varsha got bored of his mechanical answer soon. She picked out a pink bikini with a white floral print and asked him, 'I think this will look good on you if you wear it at the reception. What do you think?'

'Anything you like,' Saahil replied, without taking his eyes off Varsha. He realized his mistake only when the salesgirl who had been attending them giggled.

Even Saahil couldn't help smiling a dry smile. To be more correct, it was a wet smile that had absorbed millions of teardrops in it. Their smiles had become wet these days and tears had dried up.

They finished shopping for the wedding clothes and shoes for Saahil by that evening. Varsha asked, 'What should we do next?'

'Let's have dinner somewhere,' Saahil replied.

'Fine. Can we invite our well-wishers who have helped us to have dinner with us? I may not get a chance to thank these people in future.' Varsha regretted having said the last sentence just the next moment. She hadn't intended to sound so pessimistic. 'You know…I mean…' she tried to rectify herself in vain.

Saahil caressed her hair. 'You don't need to explain anything. We both know what you mean.'

Saahil invited Vaibhav, Makaan bhai and Mr. Das to join them for dinner at the roof top garden restaurant that they often used to go to. Winter had enhanced the charm of the restaurant. As Saahil and Varsha waited for their guests to arrive, Saahil said, 'I noticed earlier today that the guests have started to arrive for the wedding. Don't they want you to stay at home and spend time with them?'

'I don't know what they want me to do. I only know what I want to do, and I want to spend these four days of my life with you. I don't know what will happen after, but these four days are ours. No one can prevent me from being with you during these four days. Moreover, when I stay at home and witness the wedding preparations, a sense of doom engulfs me.'

'What about Mr. Dev? Doesn't he mind your staying out when so many guests are at home?'

'He doesn't care about me or my whereabouts these days. He only cares about winning the game. I don't see my brother in him these days. I have lost him to this game.' Varsha struggled to hold her tears back.

Vaibhav, Makaan bhai and Mr. Das joined them soon after. 'The celebration is regarding the new house, I suppose,' said Mr. Das cheerfully after they had ordered dinner.

Saahil said, 'Not really. Actually, Varsha wants to spend some time with all of you.' After a pause, he added, 'Perhaps, for the last time.'

The last few words made the guests perturbed. Mr. Das asked, 'Why for the last time?'

'If she marries Alok, she will have to go with him to his place,' Saahil said.

The look on Saahil's face told the guests that it was not a joke. Silence hovered over the dining table for a few moments. Then, Mr. Das said, 'I thought you fulfilled all the conditions set by Mr. Dev when you purchased the house. Why should she marry Alok now?'

'There is one more condition still left to be fulfilled. My bank account must have a balance of at least ten lakh rupees. I spent almost everything that I had to purchase the car. It's just impossible to arrange for ten lakh rupees within four days, or rather three days now.'

Silence prevailed again until Varsha tried to ease the situation. 'Hey, it's no use discussing the issue. Let's keep the topic aside and have some good time and a good dinner together.'

Makaan bhai objected, 'On the contrary, we should keep the dinner aside and focus on the issue. We can't let Mr. Saahil's effort go fruitless at this stage when he is on the verge of succeeding. I am sure there must be some way out.'

'Makaan bhai, I don't see any way out this time. All that I can see for my future now is my new empty house without Varsha,' Saahil said, his voice heavy.

'Don't worry, Mr. Saahil. I deal in houses, but I love to see them turn into homes the most. I promise you, I will do everything that I can to turn your house into a home too,' said Makaan bhai.

'Do you really think that's still possible?' A glint of hope flickered in Saahil's eyes.

Mr. Das said, 'Makaan bhai is right, Saahil. Things seem impossible until you start trying. Hadn't you thought at first that it was impossible for you to own a house? But now, you are the owner of a house. We should start thinking of possible solutions to your problem instead of wasting time thinking of an unpredictable future.'

'But is there really any solution to this problem?' Varsha asked.

Mr. Das replied, 'Of course. The best solution is to talk to Mr. Dev. I suggest that Makaan bhai and I meet Mr. Dev and try to convince him to call off your wedding with Alok, and allow Saahil some more time to fulfil the last condition. Considering the fact that Saahil has achieved so much in the last few months and has fulfilled most of the conditions asked by him, he may not turn down our request after all.'

'Yes, that's a good idea. We should try that,' Makaan bhai agreed with Mr. Das.

Varsha said, 'That will be of no use, Makaan bhai. You haven't met bhaiya recently. You don't know how much he has changed. He is very stubborn about this matter. He behaves very rudely when it comes to his decision about my marriage. I know he won't listen to your request. He will talk to you disrespectfully instead. I don't want Das uncle and you to face such humiliation.'

'So what if he insults us? That's a very small price for us to pay to see you kids live together happily, and we are ready to pay it,' Mr. Das assured them.

'Uncle, Varsha is absolutely right. Mr. Dev is in no mood to listen to anyone. It's no use trying to convince him. In fact, it may even worsen the situation. I don't want to make things more difficult for Varsha,' Saahil said.

Saahil had a valid point, so Mr. Das and Makaan bhai had to drop the idea of meeting Mr. Dev. Everyone grew silent again. The only person who had been completely silent throughout this discussion was Vaibhav. He had been busy on his cell phone all the while. Saahil noticed it and asked, 'Don't you have anything to say? Are your social media apps more important for you than your friends' lives?'

Vaibhav looked at Saahil. 'Who told you I was busy with my social media apps? You know how important you people are to me. I was searching for a solution to your problem.'

'On your cell phone?'

'Yes, I was searching the web for "How to get ten lakh rupees in a day?" I found some interesting results. We can try one of these methods to get ten lakh rupees for you in a day,' Vaibhav replied.

'Can't you ever talk sense? You want to solve my problem by searching the web?' Saahil asked.

Mr. Das said, 'Let Vaibhav tell us what he found on the web. There is no harm in listening to him.'

Vaibhav looked at everyone. 'Should I proceed?' When everyone (except Saahil, of course) nodded, he continued, 'We can rob a bank. Besides getting ten lakh rupees for now, Saahil can save money for future.' He looked at everyone expectantly, hoping for them to praise him for his farsightedness.

Everyone, except Saahil, thought it was a joke, and smiled, while Saahil, who knew that Vaibhav was quite serious about what he had just said, almost yelled, 'Sometimes, I feel that the anatomy of your gut is in reverse because whenever you open your mouth, you talk only crap.'

It took others some time to realize that it was not a joke. Vaibhav looked at them, still half-expecting them to agree to his proposal, but only saw irritation and disapproval on their faces. Then he said, 'So the idea of robbing a bank is dropped, I suppose.' He scrolled down the page he was viewing and said, 'The next idea is to kidnap someone and demand a ransom.'

Saahil was too pissed to say anything. Mr. Das interjected, 'Vaibhav, I hope you understand that we are not a gang of criminals.'

'Of course, I do, but I won't mind being a criminal to help my friends at this crucial time.'

'I appreciate your feelings, but I will appreciate it more if you give some suggestion that can be carried out without violating the law.'

'Okay, let me search some more.' He scrolled further down the screen and shouted excitedly, 'I really deserve to be called smart. I've found it. This one can be carried out without violating any law.'

'What is it?' asked Saahil enthusiastically. Others were equally curious to hear the solution.

Vaibhav flashed a winning smile and said, 'It says, you may inherit the property of a millionaire by being his/her legal heir.'

Saahil tried not to lose his temper. 'And do you mind telling me whose legal heir am I? Which millionaire will bless me with his property, and why would he do so?'

Vaibhav said, 'Oh! That is a real problem. I hadn't thought of it. So *mission property inheritance* stands cancelled. Let me see what the other options are.' He looked at his cell phone again. 'Well, this one seems possible practically. It says you can borrow a loan and keep it in your bank account to show people that you are rich.'

Saahil almost yelled, 'Please, someone take him away from here before I kill him.'

Makaan bhai's eyes sparkled with hope, however. He said, 'Wait, Mr. Saahil, you don't need to kill him. In fact, you should praise him for what he has suggested right now.'

Saahil looked at Makaan bhai. 'What do you mean?'

Makaan bhai said, 'I will explain. First, answer my question. What exactly was the fourth criterion?'

Saahil thought for a moment and said, 'Mr. Dev had said that my bank account had to have a balance of at least ten lakh rupees.'

'Was that all or was there any sub-clause attached to the criterion?'

'That was all,' Saahil replied.

'Wonderful. So that means, your bank account must have ten lakh rupees. The source of the money doesn't matter. It doesn't matter how you acquired the money – stolen or borrowed as a loan,' explained Makaan bhai.

Silence prevailed again, but this time it hid hope within it. Everyone looked at each other. Varsha was the first to smile. Her smile gradually turned into laughter as she said, 'Brilliant, that's just brilliant. There cannot be a better solution.'

Saahil, however, was not completely convinced of the ethicality of the proposal. 'Doesn't the solution seem a bit unethical?' he asked.

'Don't talk of ethics. Do you think what bhaiya is doing to us is entirely ethical? It's only a game for him. Let's play the game the way he is playing it. In this game, we are not bound to stick to ethics, we are only bound to obey the rules. What we are going to do is not against the rules of the game.'

'But...,' Saahil was still in a dilemma.

'You have to choose between your ethics and me,' Varsha made it clear.

Varsha and Saahil exchanged a silent but meaningful look before Saahil finally said, 'I choose you. It will be more unethical if I don't choose you.' He smiled and it reflected on others' faces too.

'So, what's the game plan? Where will you get the loan from?' Varsha asked.

'Game plan? You are speaking Mr. Dev's language. Do you also feel that it's just a game?' Saahil asked.

'Not really. Nonetheless, I am waiting eagerly to defeat him. I would love to see his loser-face when you finally marry me.'

'Come on, he is your brother after all. It's not a war between you two,' Saahil said.

'I know that, but can you make him understand that?' Varsha asked.

Saahil knew he couldn't, so he kept quiet.

Varsha repeated her question. 'So, where can we get the loan from?'

Makaan bhai said, 'When Mr. Saahil was trying to buy a house, he couldn't get a bank loan because he didn't have the requisite documents. The same problem will arise again, so there is no point in wasting our time going from bank to bank.'

'Where else will he get a loan from?' Mr. Das asked.

'There are people whose business itself is lending money. They don't follow the stringent rules as a bank does, but only lend money to trustworthy people. The only problem is that their interest rates are much higher than those of banks,' Makaan bhai explained.

'I am ready to pay any interest.' There was despair and desperation clear in Saahil's voice.

Makaan bhai said, 'Very well. I know a few such moneylenders. I will talk to them tomorrow. I request all of you to search for any such moneylenders from your contacts too. Please meet them tomorrow and try to convince them. It will be better if we have more than one choice. We will pick the one who charges the lowest interest rate.'

All agreed with Makaan bhai.

After the waiter had served them dinner, Vaibhav asked, 'Aren't you people forgetting something – something very important?'

'What is it?' asked Saahil.

'To thank me for my valuable advice.' Vaibhav stuffed a large piece of gravy-soaked *naan* into his mouth.

'I won't thank you for your advice. I am returning the favor by giving you another valuable advice,' Saahil said.

'What is it?'

'Don't talk while eating,' Saahil smiled.

# Chapter 17

After they returned to their hostel, Saahil asked Vaibhav, 'Do you really think I will manage to get the loan and marry Varsha? Tell me honestly.'

'I hope so. You should never give up hope. Hope always pays off.' Vaibhav changed out of his clothes, switched on the electric cooking heater and sat next to it to ward off the cold.

'Do you really mean it or are you just trying to console me?' Saahil slipped under his raggedy quilt that had become threadbare due to the hard work of cockroaches and rats.

Vaibhav said, 'I mean it. I have recently seen hope pay off. Do you remember I had told you about my ex-girlfriend?'

'You mean your expected girlfriend – the girl who was never your girlfriend?'

'So you remember. I had hoped that I would meet her again and she would be my girlfriend some day. My hope paid off finally. You have been very busy lately, so I didn't get the time to tell you that I met her again last month when I visited home.'

'Really? Did your story proceed any further?' Saahil asked curiously.

Vaibhav smiled. 'I reminded her of our last meeting and asked her whether she missed me. She said she had been thinking of me since then. We talked a lot. The next day, I told her that I loved her, and I was surprised when she told me that she reciprocated my feelings too.'

'I am surprised too,' Saahil mumbled.

'Did you say something?' Vaibhav asked.

'I said I am happy for you.'

'Thanks. So the point is that hope always pays off. Hence, never give up hope. Now, go to sleep. We will meet some moneylenders tomorrow.'

'I don't know any moneylender in the city.'

'I know a few.' Vaibhav switched off the electric cooking heater and went to sleep.

Vaibhav's ready answers never failed to surprise Saahil. He was no less than a human search engine. If one needed any information, he was always ready with it.

The next morning, Vaibhav took Saahil to a suburb of the city infamous for the high frequency of criminal activity. Such incidents were so frequent there that the local correspondents of various newspapers and television channels found it highly effective to visit the area now and then to get some spine-chilling news.

Vaibhav asked Saahil to park his car in front of a beautiful mansion. Vaibhav said, 'The mansion belongs to Mantu ji. His chief business is money-lending.'

The entrance of the mansion was guarded by two heavily built men wearing *dhoti* and *kurta*. One of them recognized Vaibhav at once, and took them to Mantu ji.

Mantu ji himself was a heavily built, six foot tall man in his late forties. His huge moustache and a large old scar along his left eyebrow added to the ferocity of his already ferocious personality. 'Hello, Vaibhav ji. What brings you here?' he asked as he offered them to sit.

Vaibhav introduced Saahil to him and told him the purpose of their visit.

'That isn't a problem at all. Ten lakhs is not a big amount,' assured Mantu ji. 'When do you need the money?'

'Today.' Saahil's eyes sparkled with hope.

'Very well, you will get the money today,' said Mantu ji.

Saahil couldn't believe that all of it was actually happening, and so easily. He thought it better to clear all his doubts beforehand. 'Do I need someone who can be a guarantor on the loan?'

Mantu ji smiled. 'Don't bother about it. I already have a lot of guarantors.' He pointed to a few heavily built, *dhoti-kurta* clad men surrounding them, all looking as ferocious as Mantu ji. 'You may call them *guarantors* or *recovery officers* or *security officers* – whatever you like. They make sure that the borrower repays the loan and repays it in time.'

Vaibhav and Saahil looked at the security officers in awe.

Saahil gathered his courage to ask the next question. 'Do I have to mortgage something?'

'No, you don't have to mortgage anything, but a hypothecation will be there.'

'What will be hypothecated?'

'What is hypothecated in case of a car loan?'

'The car, of course.'

'Exactly. What I am going to lend you is a personal loan. So what should be hypothecated in this case? Come on, guess.'

Saahil hesitated before guessing. 'The person? You mean me?'

'Wow! You are quite smart.' Mantu ji laughed like a monster. His security officers performed their duty by delivering a chorus of laughter in his support.

Saahil looked confused. 'I didn't understand.'

Mantu ji took the pains to explain (or perhaps, enjoyed the pains), 'It's simple. When one fails to repay a car loan, the lender takes possession of the car. Similarly, when the borrower fails to repay the personal loan, I take possession of the person.'

'You mean, you kidnap the person?' Saahil asked hesitantly.

'No.' Mantu ji's face looked stern.

Saahil hesitated again and guessed the worst thing possible. 'You get the person killed?'

'Oh! No, no, no, I don't get him killed. A loan should always be repaid in EMIs. So, I get the person's body parts chopped off – one part every month.' It was clear from his tone that Mantu ji wasn't joking.

Saahil and Vaibhav felt their stomachs churning.

Mantu ji continued, 'That's how I recover the capital. To recover the interest, I get one or two limbs of the person accompanying the borrower chopped off.' With a villainous smile on his face, he looked at Vaibhav.

Vaibhav felt the sudden urge to flee from the place. He still gathered the courage to ask, 'Don't you have any interest-free loan schemes?'

Mantu ji guffawed and looked at Saahil. 'Vaibhav ji has a nice sense of humor, I must say.'

'You bet. Otherwise, he wouldn't have brought me to you.' Saahil looked into Mantu ji's eyes this time.

It took Mantu ji some time to understand the sarcasm. He tried hard not to lose his temper. 'You have a good sense of humor too, but my sense of humor is not up to the mark. Leave before my security officers throw you out.'

The burly security officers advanced towards them with pure aggression in their eyes. Vaibhav caught Saahil by the arm and dragged him out of the mansion. They were in Saahil's car and out of the neighbourhood in no time.

After they had driven far enough from the place, Vaibhav asked, 'Weren't you acting too smart? Do you have any idea who you were talking to? They say that the number of criminal cases pending against him is more than his age in years.'

'So what? Does that mean he can do anything to anyone? We hadn't done anything to annoy him, but that brute doesn't know how to talk and behave. By the way, don't you have any common sense? Didn't you think twice before taking me to him? How did you expect that I would agree to his absurd terms and conditions?'

'I thought you were ready to die for Varsha.'

'Wow! Brilliant! So you had taken me there to get me killed?'

'No, that was not my purpose,' Vaibhav said casually.

When Saahil had cooled down after a few minutes, he said, 'By the way, I am ready to die for Varsha, but I'd rather live with her.'

They met a few more moneylenders that day, but all of them required Saahil to mortgage something for. The only thing that Saahil could have mortgaged was his house, but messing with one achieved target in order to achieve another did not seem like a wise decision to him, so he refrained from agreeing to the moneylenders' terms and conditions. Saahil and Vaibhav went on to meet all the moneylenders that they had heard of over the next two days, but their hard work didn't pay off.

In the evening of the second day, Saahil met Varsha. 'All was in vain,' he declared, his voice half-choked.

Varsha looked at him, her eyes blank. 'I also talked to a few moneylenders. The result was the same.'

Saahil's cell phone rang at that very moment. It was Makaan bhai. He said something to Saahil, then ended the call.

'What did he say?' Varsha asked anxiously.

'He has asked Das uncle, Vaibhav and the two of us to meet him at the restaurant in an hour.'

'Any positive results?'

'He didn't say.' Saahil informed Mr. Das and Vaibhav of the meeting too.

Makaan bhai had reached the restaurant before the others arrived.

'What should we order?' asked Varsha.

'Anything from the *tandoor*. That will take some time to get prepared and we will get more time to talk without any disturbance,' Makaan bhai replied.

After Varsha had ordered, Mr. Das said, 'I met a few moneylenders that I had heard of, but none are ready to lend the money without something being mortgaged.'

Saahil and Varsha informed him that they had faced the same problem, then looked at Makaan bhai with the hope of getting some good news from him.

'I failed too.' Makaan bhai's voice was heavy with guilt. 'I turned out to be useless.'

'You need not feel guilty. You have already done a lot for us,' Saahil said.

Varsha said, 'Saahil is right. We couldn't have come this far without your help. It's just that Saahil and I couldn't win the fight against our fate. With the wedding just one day away, it's clear what our fate has in store for us now.' Looking at Saahil, she squeezed his hand gently.

Saahil tried and failed to smile.

Makaan bhai said, 'The story is not over yet. Mr. Saahil's journey of success so far has been incredible.

His optimism and perseverance have reignited my enthusiasm. I can't see him fail at this stage when success is just one step away.'

'But nothing is left to be done. We have already tried our best,' Varsha sighed hopelessly.

'No, we haven't. We will try our best now. We tried to get the money from outsiders, but we forgot about the money that we already have with us. I spent almost all the money I had when I bought a house for myself last month. Still, I have got two lakh rupees in my account right now. I am going to transfer the money to Mr. Saahil's account right away.'

'You have already done a lot. I can't accept your money,' Saahil objected.

'Shhh. Let's not waste time in formalities. The money is not going anywhere. It will remain in your account. You can give it back to me after your wedding.'

Before Saahil could object any more, Mr. Das said, 'Though I spent almost all of my savings on my daughter's wedding, I have got about one lakh rupees with me. The money will be in Saahil's account by tomorrow.'

Vaibhav said, 'I borrowed one lakh from my father to get a new bike. I will transfer the amount to Saahil's account too. The bike can wait for a few days.'

Varsha looked down in an unsuccessful attempt to hide the embarrassment evident on her face. 'Bhaiya has been giving me very less money for my expenses since his first meeting with Saahil so that I am not able to help him financially, or to fulfil the criteria set by him. I have only got one lakh with me. I will deposit it in Saahil's account tomorrow,' she said.

'Wonderful. So that makes a total of five lakhs. We only need to arrange for five lakhs more. I will contact some of my friends and see if I can manage to borrow some money from them. I request all of you to do the same. We will be in touch. Now, I must leave so that I can meet at least a few friends today itself,' Makaan bhai said and rose from his chair.

'At least have some chicken *tikka* before you leave,' Varsha insisted.

'I will have it at your wedding. We don't have any time to lose.' Makaan bhai smiled before leaving.

Everyone at the table looked at the selfless man until he vanished from their view.

# Chapter 18

Expectations are like unfaithful lovers – you suspect them, but you love them; they don't love you, but they don't leave you either. Varsha and Saahil hadn't expected their expectations to be so unfaithful.

By the next evening, all the money promised was transferred to Saahil's account. Mr. Seth, Makaan bhai's most trustworthy source of money, had gone abroad unfortunately. Even his cell phone was not reachable. Makaan bhai managed to arrange two lakh rupees from another friend of his, yet he was too ashamed to look at Saahil and Varsha directly when he said, 'Forgive me for my overconfidence. I was able to arrange for only two lakh rupees.'

Saahil simply hugged him. He didn't have any words to thank him.

No one else had been able to arrange for any more money in such less time, though each one had tried their luck with every person they knew. They still lacked three lakhs to reach the target, with no means left to fulfil it in time. Everyone had given in to the atrocity of fate. Everyone knew what was going to happen the next day – the day of the wedding – but no one wanted to talk about it. They decided to allow Saahil and Varsha a few hours of privacy for their last evening together, and bade them goodbye.

The dawn of the next day was supposed to see Varsha in her bridal attire. Their expectations had indeed turned out to be unfaithful. Now, there was no hope, no doubt and no anxiety.

Saahil and Varsha went to take their last stroll *together* along their favorite riverside. The sand was soaked from the light drizzle that had started in the afternoon and had been continuing since then. The sky was still dark, overcast with clouds. A cool breeze carried the aroma of wet earth, and some eerie sounds originating in the adjacent jungle fell on their ears now and then.

Varsha said, 'Bhaiya must be very happy. He is going to win the game finally.'

Saahil kept a finger on her lips. 'Shhh. Right now, it's just you and me. Don't even mention anyone else. There was no past. There is no future. Everything we have is in this present. Let's not think of anything except us.'

Varsha hugged Saahil. His lips found Varsha's and they closed their eyes. It was difficult to differentiate between the raindrops and the teardrops that trickled down their cheeks. They hugged and kissed, and cried and laughed, and kissed some more, losing all track of time.

As they continued their stroll after, the light drizzle turned into a shower, and the shower gradually turned into heavy rainfall. Fat raindrops hit hard against them, drenching them to the bone. The cool breeze transformed into a fierce wind, restraining their walk. It was so forceful that they had to try hard to even maintain their balance.

Roaring like angry monsters, a loud rolling thunder accompanied by lightning tried to frighten them, but they progressed, hand in hand, against the rain, against the wind, against the thunder, as if they had decided to rebel against everything and everyone, even the forces of nature.

They continued to walk along the riverside, drenched from top to toe. Their calves ached from the effort, but they continued to walk in silence. Neither uttered a word, they didn't need to.

Their walk was brought to a halt suddenly when a few successive flashes of lightning made the rising water level of the river clearly visible. They stared at it for a few seconds, then looked into each other's eyes. Feelings were exchanged without words and a decision was made. They knew they were going to win over everyone and everything this time.

They smiled at each other, tears still rolling down their cheeks. They kissed again. Holding each other's hand, they continued walking – not along the riverside this time, but toward the river.

They progressed against the wind and the rain until the cold water of the river embraced their feet for the first time. They stopped, looked into each other's wet eyes, and kissed for one last time. Almost hugging each other, they resumed their advance into the river. The water gradually began to take them into its embrace – their ankles, their calves, their knees, their thighs and upward still.

When the water reached the level of their waists, they found it really difficult to maintain their balance anymore. Their buoyancy, the force of the water current and the wind, all tried together to lift their feet off the riverbed, but they hugged each other tightly and continued walking. They didn't allow the river to carry them away from each other. They wanted death to embrace them near their favorite spot – the place on the riverside where they had spent uncountable evenings together, dreaming of a day when no one would be able to separate them.

With much difficulty, they managed to walk on till the water reached the level of their shoulders. A few steps more and the water would be above their heads, bringing an end to all their miseries. They would win over everyone and everything. But now, they found it almost impossible to keep their feet steady on the riverbed. They struggled hard to keep themselves at the same spot, but failed. They felt being drifted away by the river current.

The pouring rain blinded their eyes. The loud thunder and splash of rain over the river surface made it difficult for them to hear anything. Still, Saahil felt like Varsha was calling his name. At first, he thought it might be a weird near-death experience. He had heard that people experienced peculiar things when they were about to die.

Yet, he continued hearing it. In spite of the rain hitting his face, he forced open his eyes to find that Varsha's lips were not moving, though he kept hearing his name being called out. The sound seemed to be coming from a distance too.

He looked toward the shore and found a human silhouette running from one spot to the next. The sound of his name was coming from that direction too. The brief flashes of lightning were not enough for Saahil to figure out who it was, but it suddenly awakened him from his foolish suicidal trance. He looked at Varsha's innocent face and thought, 'What am I doing? How could I ever think of letting Varsha die?'

He took one deep breath, gathered all his strength, held Varsha by the waist with one hand and started swimming toward the shore with the other. He took utmost care to keep her head above the water level. It was not an easy task to swim across the river in such weather, that too carrying a person along, but he succeeded.

Before Varsha could understand what was happening, they were almost near the shore, the water level receding below their waists. Soon, their feet were back on the riverbed. Saahil was panting for breath. Varsha looked at him quizzically, barely being able to make out his expression in the brief flashes of lightning.

Saahil said, 'I can never be the reason of your death.' He kissed her before dragging her along toward the shore. Varsha walked on with him mechanically. She had always loved him, but today she found him adorable.

When they reached the shore, they found the human silhouette coming toward them, still calling out Saahil's name. He was progressing hesitantly though, perhaps unsure in the dark whether the person he was approaching was indeed Saahil or not.

As the silhouette drew closer, Saahil observed that he was wearing a raincoat. Over and above that, he was also holding an umbrella, struggling to keep it in place against the fierce winds. Saahil knew only one person on earth who always used double protection against everything. He called out, 'Vaibhav, is that you?'

Fighting with the inverted umbrella, Vaibhav approached them and said, 'I searched everywhere for both of you. Then I thought you might have come here to commit suicide.'

Saahil and Varsha looked at each other guiltily, as if they had been caught stealing. After all, it was the one most shameful chapter of their life that they didn't want anyone to know about.

To their relief, Vaibhav added, 'I was just joking,' and laughed. 'I know this is one of your favorite spots, so I thought I might find you here.'

'Your sense of humor is as rotten as your comic timing. We will never commit suicide. We are not that weak,' said Saahil.

'That's true. We will never commit suicide.' Varsha wasn't sure whether she was trying to assure Vaibhav or herself.

'Anyway, what's the matter?' Saahil asked.

Vaibhav said, 'Why had you left your cell phone back at the hostel?'

'I didn't want any disturbance during my last evening with Varsha. What's the matter?'

'There is a message on your cell phone. An important one.'

'What is it? Have you got the phone with you? Show me the message.'

'Here? In the rain? Let's go to some place dry.'

They left the riverside and walked over to a shop at the nearest market. Standing under its shed, Vaibhav wiped his hands on his handkerchief and took Saahil's cell phone out of his pocket.

He showed the message to Saahil and Varsha. One look at the message, and both of them were startled. Saahil snatched the phone away from Vaibhav and read the message repeatedly to ensure that he was not mistaken. They were too shocked to say anything. A few moments passed in silence. They kept looking at each other and the message.

Finally, Saahil asked, 'What should we do next?'

Vaibhav replied, 'What an absurd question? There can be only one answer to it. Meet Mr. Dev. Right now.'

All three of them rushed over to Varsha's house which was nearby.

On the way, Saahil asked, 'Who did it? Makaan bhai?'

'No. I called Makaan bhai. He didn't do it,' replied Vaibhav.

# Chapter 19

Varsha, Saahil and Vaibhav entered Varsha's house through the back door. They didn't want the guests to see them in their drenched avatar. Varsha walked them to Mr. Dev's room.

Before entering Mr. Dev's room, Saahil read the message on his cell phone again in order to gain the confidence needed to talk to Mr. Dev. The message read, "Your account has been credited three lakh rupees. Available balance in your account is ten lakh rupees."

They didn't know where the money had come from, but that hardly mattered at the moment. That one message had changed the scenario completely within the last few minutes. Now, Saahil and Varsha had undoubtedly won the game, and Saahil was ready to ask Mr. Dev for Varsha's hand in marriage. They didn't even have the time to celebrate the success. They weren't even sure whether they should be happy yet or not, unsure whether Mr. Dev would keep his promise and call off Varsha's wedding with Alok.

Varsha knocked on the door of Mr. Dev's room and entered without waiting for his permission. 'Bhaiya, we want to talk to you. It's urgent.'

Mr. Dev looked up as the three that made up the "we" entered his room one by one. Weirdly enough, he wasn't surprised to see Saahil and Vaibhav in his room at that time of the night. He casually said, 'You people are all wet. You will catch a cold. Varsha, go and change into dry clothes, then come back. Meanwhile, Saahil and...' He looked at Vaibhav.

'This is Vaibhav,' Varsha introduced.

'Yes, meanwhile, Saahil and Vaibhav may change into some of my clothes. Then, we will talk.'

'No, bhaiya, we want to talk to you right now,' Varsha insisted.

'Do as I say.' Mr. Dev's voice sounded more stern this time. It made Varsha leave at once. She realized that she still had respect for her brother.

Mr. Dev handed Saahil and Vaibhav some towels and his clothes to put on. 'Dry yourselves and change into these. These may not fit you, but it's better than catching a cold.' He showed them to the bathroom. He called the maid then and asked her to bring coffee for all of them.

It hardly took Varsha and the boys any time to change their clothes and reappear before Mr. Dev. The maid was equally quick to bring the coffee. After the maid had left, Mr. Dev said, 'So Saahil, did you get your month's salary in advance? I had asked Kashyap to transfer it to your account today. Is three lakhs per month okay with you or do you need a raise?' Mr. Dev had a child-like mischievous smile on his face.

Varsha, Saahil and Vaibhav stared at each other, thinking that Mr. Dev had gone mad. Saahil asked,

'Salary? What salary?' but then connected the dots the very next moment. 'Hang on a minute! My account has been credited by three lakh rupees today. You mean, you sent me the money?' His voice was shaky because of confusion and surprise.

Mr. Dev said, 'To be more precise, the office of my new venture has sent you the money. I am going to own a car dealership very soon. The showroom is ready. Only a few official formalities are to be completed, and you are going to be the managing director and my partner in the venture. There is going to be one more partner – Varsha.'

Saahil stared at Mr. Dev. The smile on his face convinced Saahil that it was nothing but a demeaning joke. Saahil faked a smile and said, 'Sir, I appreciate your sense of humor, but I am very tense right now. I request you, please don't play jokes on me right now.'

Varsha said, 'Bhaiya, please don't make fun of Saahil.'

Mr. Dev stopped smiling. 'So you think it's a joke? It's not.' He sighed and remained silent for a few seconds, then jumped off his chair upon remembering something. 'Wait a minute. I have got something to show you.' He opened his cupboard and searched for something in a hurry. After a few moments of frantic searching, he took out a green file and gave it to Saahil and Varsha to look. 'Just go through it,' he said.

Mr. Dev sat sipping his coffee as Saahil and Varsha flipped through the pages of the agreement contained in the file, glancing briefly at the contents, their eyes growing wide with utter disbelief. The agreement dealt with various aspects of the partnership between Mr. Dev,

Varsha and Saahil. All the pages of the agreement had already been signed by Mr. Dev.

'The agreement is waiting to be signed by both of you. Sign it so we can complete the legal formalities and the car showroom can start functioning soon. Your chamber in the car showroom is waiting for you. You can join there as soon as possible, I am tired of working alone.' Mr. Dev finished his coffee and kept the cup aside.

To the others, everything seemed just like a dream – bodies were motionless, thoughts blocked, hearts overwhelmed at the events taking such a favorable turn on their own. It took them at least a few minutes to come to terms with what was happening and speak. Doubts still persisted. Varsha asked, 'Bhaiya, is the agreement a part of your joke?'

Now, Mr. Dev looked serious. 'Do you really think I will make a joke out of your life?'

'No.' The word slipped out of Varsha's mouth involuntarily and instinctively.

'Then why don't you believe that it's not a joke?'

Varsha didn't know what to say.

'Can I ask you something, sir?' Saahil asked.

'Yes, what is it?'

'You can easily get someone more educated and more experienced than me to work for you. Then why me?'

'Education and experience are important, but the most important factor is another word that starts with an 'e'. It's *efficiency.* One salesperson, getting a salary of ten thousand rupees per month, goes from door to door on his bicycle, selling slimming kits. Then, he quits his job and starts his own business. Within only a few months, he starts earning more than a lakh every month. He has his own house. He has a car. He has a decent bank balance. I don't know any other person who has been able to achieve so much in so less time. And as far as I know, he hasn't used any unfair means to achieve all this. Everything combined suggests only one thing – he is amazingly efficient. Why should I search for anyone else when he is here to work with me? Of course, I haven't asked for his consent till now. So Saahil, are you ready to work with me? Are you willing to be my partner in my new venture?'

Every revelation made by Mr. Dev was so stupefying that the three took their time to accept the facts, judge and speak. After a few more moments of silence, Saahil said, 'Sir, only a fool would refuse to work with you.'

'"Sir" is too formal. Now that we have become partners, it will sound better to my ears if you call me just "bhaiya" instead of "sir",' Mr. Dev resumed smiling.

Varsha's eyebrows refused to leave their raised-in-doubt stance, though she couldn't suppress a smile quickly spreading across her face. 'Bhaiya, do you really feel so about Saahil?'

'Do I need to produce proofs in support of everything I say?'

'Of course not.' The anger against her brother that had accumulated in her heart over the last few months sublimated in a matter of minutes. She even felt the instinct to go hug her brother, but refrained from doing so. The most important matter was yet to be discussed. She said, 'Bhaiya, you don't know how happy I am to see the change in your attitude toward Saahil. The offer of the partnership is incredible, but the matter that we came to discuss with you is of prime importance.'

'Oh! I totally forgot. You had come to talk to me about something. Tell me.'

'Do you remember your promise?'

'Which promise?'

'You promised that you would call off my wedding with Alok and let me wed Saahil if he fulfilled all the conditions set by you any time before the wedding.'

'Yes, I remember.'

'Saahil has fulfilled all the conditions. We can show you the proofs if you want.'

'I know he has. I have kept track of everything without your knowledge. You don't need to show me the proofs.'

'You must keep your promise now. We have won the game.'

'You had won the game right at the beginning because I was never in the game. Saahil and you were the only players in the game.' Mr. Dev leaned back in his chair.

All eyes in the room grew wide. 'What do you mean?' asked Varsha.

'I inquired about Saahil after you told me about him for the first time. Before I asked you to have him meet me, I had already decided that I would let you marry him. All this while, Saahil was only competing against himself, not against me.'

Mr. Dev thought Saahil and Varsha would be most happy to hear the revelation he had just made, but he was wrong.

'What?' Varsha rose from her chair at once. She was on the verge of crying. 'You had already decided in favor of our marriage? Still you made us suffer like this? You made us go through all the hardships and agony deliberately? Why?' She tried hard not to let her words get dissolved in her sobs.

Mr. Dev embraced her affectionately and patted her on the back to console her as she went on sobbing. 'Calm down. Calm down,' he tried to pacify her.

After Varsha had controlled her sobs, she looked at Mr. Dev to find his eyes moist too. She couldn't recall when she had last seen tears in her brother's eyes.

He made her sit beside him and said. 'I know I owe you people an explanation. I have been very rude to both of you. I didn't want to be, but it was necessary.'

Vaibhav asked, 'Why, sir?'

'Because I didn't want my sister to marry someone whose only possession was his good character, nor did I want her to marry someone of my choosing alone, someone whom she didn't love. When she told me about Saahil, I inquired about him and found out that he is a boy of immensely good character. I was happy that Varsha had chosen such a nice boy. I found out that he is orphaned too, but I didn't have a problem with that. However, his state of unemployment disappointed me. He earned very less from petty jobs at the college and the library. That amount was certainly not enough to lead a happy and decent life, that too with a family of one's own in today's world. Every brother on earth wishes for a happy life for his sister. I am no exception. I knew you two wouldn't be able to lead a happy life with his petty earnings. On the other hand, I didn't want to lose a nice boy like Saahil. Moreover, I didn't want to force Varsha to marry someone other than Saahil. Her happiness means the world to me.

'My sources had informed me that Saahil was not serious enough about his life. If I had casually asked him to do something to make a decent living, he would have taken years to do so, and I couldn't have kept Varsha unmarried for that long. I knew Saahil had great potential because he had completed his graduation without anyone's support. It's not easy for an orphan.

'I just needed a plan that would awaken the man of potential in him and trigger his enthusiasm to achieve something concrete in life. So, I put him in this do-or-die situation. I asked him to fulfil those difficult conditions in limited time. I thought he would do anything for Varsha, and I was right. Look what all he has achieved now. I also wanted to see if Varsha would continue to love Saahil in spite of enduring all the hardships, and I am proud to say that she didn't disappoint me.' Mr. Dev smiled at Varsha.

The rain had stopped by now. Only occasional thunders interrupted the silence of the night. A cold breeze swooshed in through the windows.

Varsha reached for a shawl lying on the bed nearby and wrapped it around herself. Her eyes were still not completely dry and her mind was still not completely devoid of doubts. She asked, 'What if Saahil had failed to fulfil the criteria?'

'I would have let you marry him anyway. But in that case, I might not have been as happy as I am today. I am confident now that he is capable enough to take good care of you. Today, I am sure that he is the right choice for you.' Mr. Dev smiled, looking at Saahil.

Saahil reciprocated the smile. He was feeling ecstatic that his struggles and tribulations had finally come to an end. The fact of much greater importance was that he had finally won Varsha's hand in marriage. The final result made him forget all his bitterness for Mr. Dev, but he had his own set of doubts to clear. He asked, 'Why did you search for an alliance for Varsha when you had already decided in favor of our marriage? Why did you want Varsha to get engaged to Alok?'

'Because I knew these things would act like a catalyst for you in the process of achieving the goals.'

Saahil realized that Mr. Dev was justified in doing so, but the most difficult question was yet to be answered. He said, 'Everything is set for the wedding tomorrow. Everyone must be looking forward to it. How will you convince Alok and his family members now to call off the wedding at the last moment? They will be furious.'

'No, they won't be,' Mr. Dev was confident.

'Why?'

'Because there is no one called Alok. There is no such family.'

'Whattt?' The last consonant vibrated inside Varsha's mouth, denoting the degree of her surprise.

'Yes, you heard it right. Alok is not a real person. He was only a product of my imagination. I had to create his story for the reasons that I just told you. His story acted like a catalyst for you.'

'What about the messenger who had come to our house before the engagement, and the ring he brought?' Varsha asked.

'He is an actor friend of Kashyap's. He was happy to play the messenger in my drama for a few bucks. I bought the ring and the other things that he had brought with him.'

This shocker made everyone speechless for a moment.

Vaibhav exclaimed and broke the silence, 'Wow! Wow! Sir, you are a genius.'

'No. I am just a brother,' Mr. Dev replied.

Saahil leaned back in his chair silently. Sitting in front of him was the person who had changed his life completely in a matter of only a few months. Saahil was confused whether to be angry at Mr. Dev for having made him go through all the hardship, or to thank him for having made him realize his potential and achieve the things that he would have taken years to achieve otherwise. Undoubtedly, the second emotion dominated in his mind, as was evident from the subtle smile that lingered on his lips.

Mr. Dev was sure that Varsha was not going to forgive him for what he had done with this revelation.

However, he was wrong again. Varsha freed her arms from the shawl with a jerk and hugged Mr. Dev tightly. A huge grin appeared on her face. 'Bhaiya, you are the best brother in the world. And I am the most stupid sister in the world.'

The grin gradually gave way to more tears. A few hours ago, she had been angry with Mr. Dev for all that he had done to them. Now, she was sorry for all that she had done to him. She wanted to apologise to him for her bad attitude toward him over the previous few months, but she couldn't as her sobs choked her voice. However, she didn't need to say anything. Mr. Dev understood all that she didn't or couldn't say. He caressed her head affectionately.

He let her cry as long as she wanted to, and after her tears dried, he said, 'Forget the past. Tomorrow will be a new beginning for both of you. Let's have dinner now, then we will look at some samples of your wedding invitation cards. You people will help me choose one.'

'Invitation cards?' Saahil asked. 'The wedding is tomorrow. What's the use of seeing the samples of invitation cards tonight? I thought you had already invited the guests. I saw a good number of them outside the hotel.'

'Those guests are here for the engagement ceremony. You are going to get engaged to Varsha tomorrow. The preparations going on at the hotel are for the same. The wedding ceremony has to be far more lavish, and shall take place a month from today,' said Mr. Dev.

After the barrage of surprises that evening, this revelation seemed no more than a gentle nudge. 'You seem to be in the mood of springing only surprises at us today,' Varsha smiled.

Mr. Dev smiled too. 'This was the last of them, I assure you. One's wedding is supposed to be a one-time event in one's life, and the happiest one too. However, the days leading up to it in preparation and meeting up with friends and shopping tend to be more enjoyable. I didn't want to deprive you kids of that happiness.'

Saahil and Varsha couldn't find the words to express their joy. They just went on smiling.

Mr. Dev said, 'Now, let's have dinner. I am extremely hungry.'

Vaibhav, who had been sitting quietly in thoughtfulness, suddenly said, 'I have read somewhere that sixty percent of…'

Before he could complete the sentence, Saahil forcefully shut Vaibhav's mouth with his hand and said, 'We are not interested in listening to your facts and figures.'

Mr. Dev laughed. 'Let him say what he is saying. It may be something interesting.'

Saahil said, 'The dinner would be much more interesting, I am sure.'

Laughter reverberated through the room; laughter borne out of love, joy, as well as achievement.